ESME OLIVER

SMOKE
DRINK
F ✳ #K

For more information contact:
Riverdale Avenue Books
5676 Riverdale Avenue
Riverdale, NY 10471
www.riverdaleavebooks.com

Design by www.formatting4U.com
Cover by Karen Knecht
Digital ISBN: 9781626013452
Print ISBN: 9781626013469

First edition, February 2017

If you resolve to give up smoking, drinking and loving, you don't actually live longer; it just seems longer.

Clement Freud

Acknowledgements

To my childhood girlfriends who all started reading my short stories in third grade (Autumn, Heather, Lynn, Colleen, Julie, Diane) and are still reading them now, in my middle age. To my grown-up girlfriends who always read my silly blog and who have read drafts of this story and many others (Trina, Susan, Melissa, Jill, Terri, Ann, Lee, Ilyse, Alicia, Jessica, Liz, Margarita, and Gwen).

To my first brilliant boss Sara who taught me how to write and told me what I needed to be reading. You taught me so much. To another brilliant boss Dinah who pushed me hard in many dimensions and also helped me refine my writing.

To Mario Correa for helping me write my first pitch to the agents. To my amazing and talented book cover designer Karen Knecht for your vision. To my diligent editors, Laurie Horowitz and Roz Weisberg, who made this book a whole lot better. To my agent Lori Perkins who always believed in this book. Special thanks to my consummate editor and dear friend, Ann Williams who made everything sharper and sexier. To my bestie Jeff for his constant emotional (and at time, financial) support. Finally, to my parents for always pushing me so hard to write and to never give up.

Chapter One

I am turning 40.

As any 39-year old woman can attest, this rite of passage, this voyage to a new decade now known as "middle age" generates... well, some variation of unbridled panic.

I do not like new decades. I did not like turning 30 either. In fact, I had a meltdown. I kept asking myself, *where did my 20s go? What have I really accomplished? What do I really want to be when I grow up (which is right now by the way)?*

At 30, I was a lawyer, and knew I wasn't a lawyer. It just wasn't me, and I had known that for a very, very long time. So finally, I quit... kind of with plans to move to New York City and kind of with no plan at all.

So upon turning 30 I had no career at all, despite all the hard work, good grades and student loans that I had amassed to obtain one. My much older uber-successful Wall Street boyfriend and I had just broken up because I wouldn't move to China where he was to be stationed on a corporate assignment for five years. Oh, and also because he was depressed and lonely when he was with me and depressed and lonely when he was without me.

Or so he said. It was just impossible to make him happy, and I grew tired of trying to do so.

The day before I turned 30, my hairdresser told me I had to go back to dark brown hair. The carmel color I was so fond of was destroying my hair, and he refused to highlight it anymore. And so with that transition to Joan Jett black at the precipice of turning 30, I looked 40. It doesn't seem significant to you. But changing your hair color around a big birthday can be quite a traumatic event.

But the real meltdown occurred when I came home from my last day at work at the big boring law firm to find a card from my almost non-existent grandmother: "You are 30! You old gal! Happy birthday!"

I threw myself on my bed and cried for an hour.

I guess I never realized how young I really was back then. I just knew I was losing a great decade of fucking unbridled fun with very little responsibility. And my future remained unknown. Completely unknown.

My view was that it was time to grow up, have a real career and flush 401(k) and maybe even start thinking about having a family. I just had no idea how to get there, and I wondered if I ever would. So far things hadn't turned out at all like I had planned and expected.

I've never dealt with uncertainty well. I've always been the type to have a plan.

Now, on the cusp of 40, I ask myself: *Where did my 30s go? And is this really where I saw my life being at this time?*

No fucking way.

We are Gen X. We were raised to believe that men and women are equal and that with hard work and good grades, you could accomplish anything. *You could have it all.* But then here you are at 40, and you learn that men actually do make more than women. And you don't have three kids like your mother did, and you aren't even a VP yet because there's this thing called the glass ceiling and the "Baby Boomers" who just aren't retiring. Your "house" is actually a condo and much much smaller than the one you grew up in. You don't have a husband, and your boyfriend is an ass. This is not how it was supposed to turn out—at all. Did our parents and teachers just feed us one big lie? Or did we really think it was possible to have it all by the time we turned 40? Is there anyone out there who does? Does Hillary Clinton just think I'm going to keep listening to and believing that "anyone" can obtain the "American Dream?"

Despite this misleading fantasy world perpetuated by my parents, I decide, like all things in life I take on, this year before this dreaded birthday, I will embrace it and take it on as a challenge.

I decided I would prepare. At the onset of age 39, I began a series of purported age-defying, self-improvement measures: Yoga, Pilates, YogaLites, Running (5ks, 10ks, interval training), Glycolic peels, highlights, low lights, Brazilian Keratase treatments, Brazilian waxes, laser hair removal...

I vowed to eliminate the crows' feet suddenly emanating from my temples and fill in the recessed purple circles expanding underneath my eyes. To eradicate that furrowed brow (most likely attributed to too many years of squinting at my asshole bosses for their inappropriate and probable sexually harassing comments). To clean up the cellulite on my ass (More running? Creams with massive doses of caffeine?), and skim the icing off the muffin top that is there on account of the kiloliter of wine I consume each and every night. This year, I told myself, it's going to be different.

I am going to look amazing at 40.

Yet as I got closer and closer to 40, and as everyone told me that I looked great for my age, I just didn't believe them. And as I looked in the mirror, a few weeks before turning 40, I realized, after all this prep work, I looked exactly the same as I did last year. And the year before. I will always be, more or a less a size 6. If I eat a little too much, I will creep up to an 8. If I eat very little, I will drop to a size 4.

I guess one could argue that this mission was driven by gross insecurity. But I don't think that is the case. I mean, that could be one component of it. Admittedly, I've never contended that I am the most secure and well-adjusted girl. I think that most of the aforementioned measures were taken because: i.) I am a perfectionist and pretty hard on myself (as a lot of girls are; it's a very hard world for girls these day) and ii.) I just wasn't anywhere near where I thought I would be at this age and iii.) I was hoping these minor self-improvement measures would make things a little better.

In sum, I just didn't have my house in order.

However, despite all the concerted effort and myriad treatments, nothing much changed in my appearance over the course of this year except maybe evidence of some barely discernable indentations in my deltoids.

Not only had my appearance barely changed over the course of the last year, my relationship status had not changed much either. I never seem to have the boyfriend or the big fucking present on my birthday. In fact, I think guys deliberately break up with you before big events like birthdays or Valentine's Day because they just don't want to shell out the cash.

My boyfriend and I just broke up.

There are lots of rules that I just can't follow. I've never been good at structure nor authority. And I don't like being pushed around.

There is life that will exist only on his terms.

There is no room for me to breathe.

There is the sex that isn't good anymore.

There are the constant comparisons to his ex-wife.

EXHIBIT A:

A huge fight that is unnecessary precipitated by a question from him about what girls talk about with each other.

"Well. What do you and Allison talk on the phone about? I mean do you guys talk about the stock market crash or investing your money at all?" He asks me one gloomy day as we languished on the couch reading newspapers and magazines.

Earlier that day, I guess he had heard me on the phone with my friend, Allison.

"No," I stretch my legs on the couch and flipping through my iPad reading *The New York Times* and *The Washington Post.* I kind of already know where this one is going.

"You don't?" He asked in an alarmed voice.

"No." I flip to the next article and start pouring

through the article about End of Life Care for your parents, which has been a subject of interest to me since I found out my father has blown a shitload of cash recently and is not in the best of health. Plus, I need a diversion. I feel a really big fight is about to come on.

"Well, what *do* you guys talk about?"

"Henry, *you* know what we talk about." Where are my cigarettes? I need a fucking smoke. But he doesn't know I'm smoking again.

"No, I don't. I really don't. Tell me."

I throw the iPad down on the sofa.

"We talk about what all girls talk about—our jobs, our boyfriends, our weight, the best under eye cream, the best concealer, shoes…. You know all this. What all girls talk about!" I assert confidently.

"Not *all* girls talk about that." He says calmly and smugly.

"Yes. They do. I'm a girl. I would know."

"Not all girls."

"Henry, I work with women of all ages and of all backgrounds, and yes they do talk about this. Women who are like 60 years old sometimes come up to me and compliment me on my shoes and ask me where I got them. I know what women talk about!"

"That's what *you and your friends* talk about."

"Ok. You give me one example of a woman that doesn't talk about these kind of things."

"I know one."

"Who?"

"My ex-wife."

The Hiroshima bomb again—the ex-wife.

"How in the hell do you know what that crunchy

6

granola ex-wife talks about with her friends? That's the point! We don't tell you what we talk about with our girlfriends!"

"I just know she didn't care about those kind of things."

"Ok, Henry! Point taken. I'm vacuous and stupid, and she is substantive and above the fray… she would never ever talk about things like shoes or under eye creams."

"I don't think you're stupid. You read more than anyone I know. If you were stupid, do you think I'd hang out with you?"

I feel like I'm going to start crying. I don't know what he wants me to be. On one hand, he wants me beautiful and rail thin and in high-priced clothes, but on the other hand, he makes fun of every effort I take to get there. Then I feel the familiar overwhelming cloak of self-doubt creeping in. Maybe I am vapid. Maybe other girls really don't care so much about what they look like, and I just should be more focused on things like saving the whales (the ex-wife's pet cause).

"You think I'm shallow. You're always telling me how much money I spend on facials or manicures. Don't think I don't notice it. And I am really sick of hearing about your ex-wife."

I get up and slam the bedroom door. And this is how it starts to go with us and the invisible but always present ex-wife who I am compared to constantly and reminded that I don't measure up to her.

There are a lot more fights. There are few explanations. In fact, to this day, I'm not really sure who dumped who.

We're not going to make up or get back together. It's just too complicated, and the whole thing is just too depressing.

There will be no flowers on the dreaded day.

There will be no presents.

There will be no surprises.

And of course, that ass does all this right before my 40th birthday and right before I'm supposed to go on an overseas trip to celebrate the same.

I am going to Italy in three days.

I do not want to go.

There is the pressure at work that is increasing each day—the pressure to get a huge chunk of change from the Department of Defense when the mercurial Congress has decided to do massive spending cuts and eliminate all "earmarks." I also know that even though the Republicans' sudden decision to cut all discretionary spending is not my fault nor remotely within my control, I will be held accountable for this and probably not get my bonus.

About six months ago, I gave up my high profile high-paying job in DC as a high tech lobbyist to return to Indiana where I grew up to work for a nonprofit. I was utterly and completely burnt out of my job in DC as well as my loser boss who often referred to me as a sorority girl and commanded me to organize wine tastings. I was sick of him drawing pictures of my head with question marks in it and telling me I couldn't find solutions to problems. Although I had graduated at the top my class from law school and worked for men who had run for president of the United States, on a daily basis, I was being told I was stupid, and I started to think that everyone was starting to believe him.

And right before he started that shit, the hoodlums in DC came after me for my purse and shot at my boyfriend and I seven times as we were walking home from the movies one Thursday night. I don't know what a nervous breakdown looks like or how you know if you are really having one. But I might have had one at 39. I mean I must have if I just got up and left (without even selling my house) and moved to fucking Indiana. But here I was. Turning 40, treading water, making little progress at this rinky-dinky nonprofit out in the middle of the Midwest.

Jesus. I'd once thought I'd be the Vice President of Government Relations for Apple at 40.

In addition, at our office, there are all these Gen Y slackers who don't do their work or meet their deadlines, which by the way is affecting my "written goals" and jeopardizing my fucking bonus. They called Gen X "slackers," but weren't we the ones who took internships for no pay, worked late nights and weekends, sacrificed our social lives, "work outs" and having kids for our "careers?" Generation Y wants to know what other people make, how soon they can become "Directors," and how soon they can get out the door to go to yoga fusion. They "text" you that they are running late, never meet deadlines which they blame on your "failure to communicate," and *tell* you when they are taking a vacation. Good Lord. I would have been fired ten times over for this, but they don't care. They view the world in different lenses. They know we all got laid off from Microsoft or lost our jobs on account of corporate mergers and acquisitions or a sudden downturn in the economy. Why work all these hours? Why be loyal? They witnessed the rise of

Mark Zuckerberg and millionaire athletes and wanted all those riches. For them, the world is as instant as the grammar free worlds of instant messaging, Twitter and Facebook. They constantly post photos on Facebook of their latest exploits as if the paparazzi are following their every move. For them, there is no honor in working 40 years for a pat on the back and a swift kick in the ass. For them, the honor's in the dollar. It's Gen Y; it's Gen Me. And they may have a point.

I start to just give up on the entitled kids at my office who grew up getting awards for participation. I've never been good at making people do what I want them to do anyway. I become disappointed, and then I become angry and irritable. Then I squint. Then I need more Botox. As a result, I have learned to rely on myself. My standards are high. And I meet them.

And I'm under all this pressure to fundraise and secure funding from the government and foundations so our organization can continue to exist, and no one is helping me. I find and write all the grants, and this wasn't even supposed to be my job. But the grant writer I hired told me recently she actually isn't a "writer" of grants, she's a "manager" of them. She also can't be counted on to do much managing. Last week, as we were about to present to a major donor, she bolted out of the office to go home and deliver her alpaca's babies. I'm not kidding. Who leaves work to go deliver the offspring of cattle?

I'm out here in the middle of nowhere. I need a life vest.

And I left DC for all this hilljack nonsense.

At work, I have a ton of things due all at once. I don't feel like it's a good time to leave for two weeks.

And I know my boss is going to be very pissed off that I'm going. He never takes vacations of any kind. Our number two tells me that I have to take my iPad and log on as soon as I get to Rome and also in the countryside of Umbria even though the wireless never works there. Jesus. I'm working at a dinky nonprofit not Microsoft. I'm really NOT that important, and there is nothing monumental going on here.

There is also the knowing that it was a very very bad idea to travel with my uber-anal retentive and controlling friend Jackie. I just know we were going to get into a fight. And I know this all in advance of the trip—but I just can't get out of it now.

"Do you have your passport? A photocopy of your passport? You really need to do that. I know we get a free breakfast at the hotel in Rome, but I'm going to bring kashi. I'm also packing sweaters in case it gets cold a night. Did you pick up *Frommer's*?"

She starts the analness on the phone. I feel like I'm dealing with my mother. Jackie kind of talked me into this trip at a weak moment. She made me book the ticket to Rome one night after I had many cocktails with my wild girlfriends. Not a good way to start a trip.

There is the asphalt gray wet sky protruding through the wide-open sunroof of my car, and the reservoir of emptiness in my heart post-Henry... the feeling that everything is suddenly going wrong again. I drive around aimlessly crying not because I know he is right for me but because in some way, I will really miss him, and I dread being alone again.

These days I'm always tired—moving like molasses with barely any energy. It's all I can do to get up and go to work.

But I know that I must snap out of it. I know I must rally and go to Italy have some fucking fun.

I walk into a boutique near my office that I frequently visit for small doses of retail therapy that is allegedly supposed to quiet the noise in my head and assuage the pain in my heart. The manager says to me:

"What's wrong? Your eyes are red!"

"My boyfriend and I just broke up."

"Oh, my God. I'm so sorry."

She tucks her long straight black silky hair behind her ear.

She folds a cute kelly-green sweater into a perfect square, and I immediately start to covet it. Even in my darkest moments, I can shop and find happiness in beautiful clothes. I peel a retro jean jacket off the hanger and evaluate it from all angles.

"And I'm turning 40 in three weeks."

I rub my hands over my recently Botoxed forehead and sigh.

"Really? Oh, my God! You do *not* look 40."

"Thanks."

Everybody tells you that you don't look 40 when your turning 40. But somehow it doesn't help. *You are turning 40, and you're starting to look it.*

I sigh, looking around the store with random, disconnected eyes. I can't focus on anything.

"And I am taking a trip for my birthday, and we're leaving in three days, and I'm not even excited." I aimlessly thumb through some antique earrings on the glass countertop.

"Where are you going?"

"Italy."

"Italy? Oh, my God! Have you read *Eat, Pray*

Love??? You *have* to read that book. You can meet a guy there and write a story."

I snap like a dry twig in the desert.

"I did read it. I hated it." I pick up an orange leather purse and spin it around.

"Really?"

"Don't get me wrong. I really liked Elizabeth Gilbert's earlier works. I was a huge fan of *Stern Men.* But I found *Eat, Pray, Love* trite and contrived. Plus, I don't know if you know this," I whisper, as if this is classified information, "but she got paid in advance by *GQ* to write it. Hardly a true-life experience. I mean... couldn't you eat pray and love for a year if someone paid you to do it? Please."

"But I loved it

"Well, I still think you could meet a guy there. Now that you're free of the boyfriend; you can write a story!"

I really hate optimistic people who always try to turn lemons into lemonade and find the best in every situation. Seriously, we just broke up two weeks ago. It really sucks. Can't you just acknowledge that fact instead of trying to spin this around into something positive? Can't you just give me two weeks to grieve and feel sorry for myself?

But she does have a point. This is good idea actually. Maybe I *should* write a book.

I have had a fairly successful blog for years and many short stories just sitting on my computer.

I leave without making a purchase. The happily-married-with-two-kids-always-chipper manager probably thinks I am a bitter jaded pill. But actually, I'm just utterly drained. Myriad phone conversations with the ex resulting in a painstakingly slow breakup have left me totally depleted. He is a vampire, and all the blood once pulsing vibrantly in my veins has been completely drained.

My niece is also a relentless optimist and always finding new options for me.

Later that evening I lay on the sofa in my parents' house, red wine in hand, trying to zone out and watch *The Unbearable Lightness of Being* for the third time. I like that it is so depressing, and I have watched the movie too many times. Suddenly, my six-year old niece, Gabriella, enters the house and jumps on my lap. Fucking disappear kid, please. Please.

"Play with me! Play with me Esme!" she demands ruthlessly. "I want to dress you up as a princess. Come on."

"Gabby," I slug back my wine. "I can't play right now. Can't you see I'm sad?"

"Why are you sad?"

"Because my boyfriend and I just broke up, Gab. And that makes me sad."

I always talk to her like an adult. She might as well know it now that most men are a dismal disappointment. I'm not going to lead her to believe that her favorite story, Cinderella, is remotely realistic.

"Don't be sad. Just go find another one!" Her big brown eyes are full of hope and optimism.

"It's kind of hard to find another one, Gab."

I chug the wine again. I contemplate putting it in a Sippy cup so it appears to be apple juice. My nieces have been seeing me belt quite a bit of wine as of late. I fear they will be in therapy one day for my drinking problem.

"No, it's not! You can find one at Target today. Just go up to a boy you think is cute and talk to him."

"I don't think I'll find at guy at Target."

"You will. You will! You'll find another one!"

She is very confident that Target contains handsome eligible men in my socioeconomic bracket.

I decide to take the advice of a six-year old.

I am going to find another one. (But not at Target).

And as my best gay friend George always says, the best way to get over a guy is to get another one. From here on out, I'm going to operate like a gay man. Find myself a pool, a cool cocktail and a Mauricio/Fabio in Italy ASAP.

And with respect to the rage for *Eat Pray Love*, here's the thing:

First of all, why eat?

If you smoke, you don't need to eat because you won't even be hungry. And smoking amps up the metabolism. Just another bennie. And why in hell would I put on 15 pounds in Italy to get over some guy? Fuck that noise. I'm not giving him *five* fucking pounds. There will be no gelato and Spaghetti Carbonara for me. There will only be tabaccheria (smoke shop) and vino rossi (red wine). I figure I can still consume two bottles of Chianti and maintain a respectable 1600 calories/day. I mean, I did not go to all the above-referenced exercise classes for an entire year to lose my barely visible obliques to Spaghetti Bolognese and Parmesan cheese.

Praying. It is an endeavor that has generated inconsistent results for me at best—and one that does not merit pursuing. And there certainly is no need to "meditate" and/or do yoga. All I think about in yoga is how I could be using this precious hour of my limited time to run off the cellulite off my ass rather than stretch it. And if I want to "calm my mind," I'll just pour myself a big glass of red wine and whip out my vibrator.

Finally, and most importantly, there is certainly no need to "love." Good Grief. This quest for love, endless love, the kind you see in the movies, has landed me right here again. Fuck love. Love is for the foolish—or perhaps the very very lucky.

And if you think I am going to cry myself through every scene of my life like Liz Gilbert did in the movie over her one failed relationship, you really are crazy. Try 20 failed ones on for size, Liz. Now there's something to cry about.

I prefer to go my own way of hedonism and self-destruction.

I'm going to go to Italy, and I'm going to *smoke, drink, and fuck.*

Come on. Doesn't this sound more fun that eating praying and loving?

If it does to you, come on *my* journey. Let's go.

Chapter Two

As I prepare to fly to Rome, my parents, the only true constant in my life, hand me the new iPhone7—the gift I have been coveting. (At 30, they gave me a Palm Pilot. I am a woman who must always be wired at all times).

Then, as now, I was dating an older, incredibly regimented, anal retentive, "me-equals-all needs-you equal-no-needs" man. Both perfect on paper, Ivy League educated, extremely successful men. One with a place in the Hamptons, one with a place in an affluent part of Virgina. Both of them taught me all about music and movies and art and fine wines. Both of them made me workout. *A lot.*

Both also had a book of edicts:

The first: Must run daily, the six-mile outer loop of Central Park (even if 20 degrees outside). Must eat bok choy and scallops and never order chips at a Mexican restaurant. Must not go out too long or too hard with your girlfriends. Must move to China with me where you will have nothing at all to do with your life—but I will make Senior Executive Super VP, and that's what's important.

The second: Must go to the gym every single day for 60 of cardio minutes—at least. Must not drink very much. Must give me orgasms even though I don't give you orgasms. Must go to bed at 10:00 p.m. Must not eat Thai (too many carbs). Must not eat pig because they are highly intelligent animals (but it's okay to eat chicken and turkey). Must not spend the night with me when restful sleep is required. Must love dogs. Must be fashionable and sexy—but absolutely effortlessly so.

One broke up with me three weeks before 30.

The other three weeks before 40.

Both contended they "*needed to be alone.*"

Actually, it's amazing how little has changed in my life over the course of ten years—except, of course, the technology upgrade.

The second one (the current one), Henry, was, however, terribly impressive and as such, seductive. He is a lawyer-doctor hybrid, super smart, incredibly witty, handsome, fashionable, Argentinian, an aficionado of music and Indie films. And I can talk to him. I *can really talk to him.* We talk for hours every single night.

Come on. That's hot. You can kind of see now why I might have put up with so much crap for so long.

I mean really, where could you find a guy like that again?

Actually, Henry found me. He pursued me. He set the pace. He always told me that I was beautiful and that I smelled good and I cracked him up. He took me away to New York City for an amazing weekend at a high-end hotel chock-full of activities at art museums, record stores, Central Park strolls, and fancy restaurants.

Also, every single day, he called me at noon while I ate my lunch at my desk and at night at eight after I had eaten my dinner. We talked about everything: our impossible sisters, politics, the state of the world, music, art, literature, and we made fun of everyone we worked with and hated. Being with him felt like hanging out with your best girlfriend.

However, looking back, I see that we talked mostly about him. His cases at work. His fucked up childhood. His recent diagnosis of fibromyalgia and all the pain in his joints. His workouts. His carefully orchestrated meal planning. His beloved dog that he called "Handsome" (which, in retrospect, is really quite gay).

He is order; I am chaos. He is regimented; I'm all over the place.

He wants to take his dog to get sheared at eight in the morning; I want to lay in bed hung over and have sex again. He uses Quicken; I use my memory to balance my checkbook… or do a transfer from savings to checking.

He is everything right that is wrong with me.

When we started dating, I thought he must be the most interesting emotionally available man I have ever met.

I was wrong. Slowly and gradually, almost without effort, he pushed me away. Ah, the saboteur. I know his tricks so well because I am the penultimate saboteur myself. I know well how to destroy just about anything that is good for me. But alas, he beat me to it.

After we hit the 3.5-month point, we had the "conversation." You know the one I mean—the one you have at three months, and if the relationship lasts, at six months, and then later at nine months.

Where is this going? Are we on the same page? Are we getting too serious?

He says:

I just feel like we're fighting all the time.

You're not happy. You're picking fights with me.

I feel "pressure."

I feel like we're getting too serious.

Blah blah. You know how it goes. It's always the same. Passive aggressive measures taken to facilitate an efficient and expedient break up—but orchestrated in a manner that makes you feel like you are the dumper not the dumpee. If it happens this way, it will assuage his guilt. He didn't want to compromise on anything. He didn't want to sacrifice. He simply did not want to commit. *I wasn't worth it.*

We had been planning to meet in California for my birthday where I would be attending a conference for work. But suddenly, he was so busy at work, he just doesn't know if he can commit to the trip. And he doesn't like to be in the sun. *And he just doesn't want to feel pressured.*

"No. No. *You* are not pressuring me, but I still *feel* pressure." He reassures me.

In any event, after two weeks of tortuous circular conversations with him, I capitulate. I mean, I can take on any J.D. or MBA—but an M.D. slash J.D.? Come on. I am not that formidable of an opponent.

He argued better than me in every case.

Voila! It is over, and although sad, in many ways, I suddenly feel *free*.

* * *

Jackie, one of my best friends, is my travel companion. We could not be more opposite, and I just know this is going to be a problem.

Just like Henry, she is controlling, anxiety ridden

and hyper-organized. She arrives at the airport with guidebooks, maps, directions, two copies of her passport and driver's license. I come with *Allure, my iPad* and a few trashy novels. I have been to Italy before, and I never read the guidebooks then. I'm certainly not going to read those things now. I want to wing it.

Query: How in the hell do I attract these anal retentive types? I am a free spirit. I eschew structure, rules and convention. I mean, these people must enrich my life in *some wa*y because I certainly gravitate toward them.

At the Atlanta airport, we have an hour to spare. We pound some big beers at the Sam Adams bar—one of my favorite airport haunts. I get an email that I had a huge victory at work, and although pleasantly surprised, my heart still hurts. I keep thinking that I will never talk to Henry again and how hard that is going to be for me. Who will I complain to about that dinosaur lady at work who glares at my high heels and refuses to answer any of my emails? Who will I run to when the Gen Y'ers fail to meet another deadline? Who will send me CDs of obscure bands in the mail?

"Listen," I tell Jackie as I belt my last gulp of beer.

"I'm telling you this now. When I get to Italy, I'm going to do three things: s*moke, drink and fuck a guy*. That's it. Then I'm going to write a story about it."

"You haven't smoked in three years! Are you serious?"

"As soon as we land in Rome, I'm buying a pack of smokes and pouring a Prosecco. Then, I'm finding

21

myself a Fabrizio. Just so you know. This is what I am doing."

She bites her lip, looks down at the bar and shakes her head.

"As long as you don't 'fuck' in front of me."

"I won't fuck in our room. I promise."

I down my beer. We are running late.

We dash to the gate—almost missing the flight which is, of course, my fault. I always almost miss flights. I also procrastinate writing papers and paying my bills. But, come on, there is something exhilarating about waiting until the absolute last minute.

Chapter Three

Rome

We land in Rome in the very early morning. Neither one of us has slept a wink on the plane. Jackie needs a cappuccino. I need some smokes. She also needs plain yogurt for the kashi she has carried onboard. WTF? In Italy, they eat little cookies for breakfast. We're in Rome. When in Rome, do Roman stuff. Not this U.S. prescriptive seed diet. Jesus Christ.

I ignore her. Turn *Sweet Emotion* on my iPod and walk right up to the Tabaccheria and order two packs of Marlboro Lights. Ah, Marlboro Lights, my old boyfriend, bad bad but always available. Always there waiting, ready to take me back.

"Are you getting cigarettes *right now*?" She sounds like my mother.

" Let the games begin!" I exclaim.

"Can you smoke in here?"

"Fuck yeah. Everyone in Italy smokes at the airport. They smoke everywhere."

It is August. It is oppressively hot, crowded, laden with tourists and super expensive due to the Euro kicking the dollar's ass. I've been to Rome before. It was Jackie who insisted we spend a few days in Rome first. I could have skipped the whole fucking city I am a girl who relishes the countryside, and that is where I feel my adventure will begin.

In Rome, Jackie isn't sleeping much, and she is always complaining about the heat and how the air conditioning in our hotel is not working. Her stomach hurts. Her head hurts. She has her period, but maybe not. She has cramps. I give her Advil. I give her Midol. I turn up the AC. Why am I the one who is always trying to pacify the anals?

Take a pill, you fucking Pill.

I want to shop. I want to meet people. Particularly male people. I want to eat pistachio gelato at sidewalk cafes and just stare at Italians walking by—women in black high strappy heels with beautiful oversized purple leather handbags, men in tailored dark jeans and boxy black blazers. I want to peer in and look at everything in oversized windows. I want to buy lavender cowboy boots that I see in one of the windows.

She, however, wants to go to the Vatican and look at all the pictures of Mary and Jesus and throw coins in the Trevi Fountain. I'm so done with the Madonna and babe thing. And I'm not interested in trying to be Audrey Hepburn by tossing pennies into water.

She convinces me go to this overpriced British chain restaurant Harry's, and take a picture in front of it because that is where Audrey Hepburn and Frank Sinatra used to hang out. If I wanted this vacation, I could have just gone to Planet Hollywood in New York City and hopped on the Big Apple tour bus.

As I approach a boutique with beautiful sundresses reaching out toward me from the window, Jackie refuses to go in and tells me she doesn't want to shop and spend money.

"I'm not going in there. I'm not shopping."

"Why not? It's August. *Saldi.* Everything is on sale!"

"I'm living on my savings now, and I'm not going in." Jackie abruptly tears down the hill and starts taking more pictures.

All I want to do is smoke, drink, fuck... and have some fun. I see Gucci, Pucci, Zegna, Sergio Rossi. The best of worldwide fashion all here ten paces from the Spanish steps. I can't stop. I buy a handbag, three dresses, a pair of camel leather gloves. I am an ugly, ugly American. Avoiding the Coliseum, the Forum and the Vatican each day to smoke, drink and shop.

Jackie and I start to argue about each day's agenda. Every single day.

So, we decide to separate. I go to an amazing new art museum focusing on "space" that makes no sense to me, but I like that it is kind of random and obscure. I have a long luxurious lunch alone with my iPad + iPod + 3 Proseccos + 1 caprese. Heaven. No one is talking to me, pulling at me. I can do whatever I want whenever I want. I meet men. I smoke cigarettes. I take long walks alone and buy more shit.

At night, in a pouring rainstorm, my former colleague and dear friend, Francesca, comes to our hotel and picks us up in her swank red shiny Alfa Romeo. Wow. She is olive, recessed in frame, and glamorous in short black tight cotton shorts with gray suede boots that move up and down into different lengths. I love them. Like all Italians, she is tiny. And glamorous and proud of her appearance. There are no "go to Target in plaid pajama bottoms, gray oversized sweat shirts with no makeup moms" here in Rome.

She takes us to the outskirts of Rome to a restaurant in the Meatpacking District that there is no way we would have ever found, and she orders everything for us. Antipasto, rich white cheeses, pasta drenched in fresh red and yellow tomatoes, soft roasted eggplant with flecks of basil, roasted vegetables, and then of course, biscotti and champagne for dessert. I can barely move.

Francesca tells us how she just ended an 11-year relationship with her boyfriend, Stefano, when she was on the cusp of turning 40.

Pretty ballsy stuff.

"I don't know. It's just not possible to date in Italy. All of these men—they are like ghosts. They disappear. Or they are married and just looking for a fling, but nothing that lasts." She tells me.

"It's kind of like that in the States too." I state.

Jackie chimes in. She never dates. She gave up on men 20 years ago when her "college" boyfriend cheated on her. She is a total manhater.

"That's why I don't date. They're all dicks. It's not worth it. I'm happy being alone." She continues. This is always her diatribe—how content she is to be alone.

"I understand. It seems useless. Now, I just travel alone." Francesca says.

I'm getting really fucking depressed, partially because I feel and believe wholeheartedly that this is what is my life is going to be like in the post-Henry era. I'm here to smoke, drink and fuck, and I don't want my mission to be aborted by talk of love had and love lost and failed relationships. They are buzzkilling my fucking vacation.

"I don't think it's natural to want to be alone. Human beings are naturally packers. We travel in packs. I don't believe that you are so 'happy' being alone." I state.

I am getting annoyed with Jackie and her false assertions.

"That's because you have never been happy being alone. You are boy crazy.

You always have been."

"Because I like men? Because I like having a boyfriend? I would say that is normal, Jackie."

"Do you regret breaking up with Stefano?" Jackie changes the subject turning to Francesca.

"No. No. I don't." She lights up her eighth cigarette.

"Really? You don't miss him?" I light one of her cigarettes.

Why am I asking these crazy questions? She is sucking me into this.

"No. Not anymore." She exhales.

"Why did you break up?" I inhale.

"Well, it's complicated." She twirls the bottom of her glass of red wine and looks toward the stained glass window on the left.

(I will later learn that "it's complicated" is a polite Italian phrase for "it's none of your fucking business, and I don't want to talk about it." You learn to shut up when the phrase "it's complicated" comes out of the mouth of an Italian.)

27

"But, well, I just always felt that I had to adapt to his life. Do you know what I mean? I mean I had to do what he wanted, and adapt to him. He was never going to adapt to my life, to what I wanted."

"Yes!" I swig my Prosecco. "I understand. This is exactly how I felt. Clearly, this is an international problem."

Are men really like this across trans-Atlantic boundaries? Do they all really want us to be little chameleons changing and adapting to their world? Don't they want to learn anything new? Aren't they interested in what we like and care about? Or are we are just supposed to be a welcome appendage to their bodies moving indiscernibly and quietly through the night operating like well behaved children—seen, but never heard?

I feel for her deeply. It is a problem without a solution. In sum, I guess you either settle and are miserable because your needs are never ever met. Or you are alone and miserable because you never did find true love. God. This is so unbelievably depressing.

But I will tell you this. I will not date another C3PO. No more Mr. Roboto.

And… I need to get the fuck out of Rome.

* * *

After four not-fun days in Rome, I am starting to really question the merits of taking this whole fucking trip.

Jackie and I get in our first of a series of fights at the Rome airport where we are picking up the *one* "automatic car" in Europe. The Golf VW we have rented has one headlight burnt out. Jackie refuses to drive it and gets into a huge fight with Angelo, the EuroCar guy. She

28

tells him that in the U.S. she would get a ticket for driving with a burned out light. She demands a new car. There isn't one. Then, she makes a movie on her phone of all the barely visible scratches and dents.

Angelo, the rental car guy gets pissed off. He has had enough.

"We are not in the U.S., Lady. They do not care here. You will be okay! No one cares."

He throws his hand up in the air and walks away.

He is *yelling* at her. Passionately, full of vitriol. I love it. In the U.S., you'd get a lawsuit slapped on you for treating the customer like this. But here you can totally go off on people, even the customers. I sit calmly in the passenger seat of the car and try to chillax and let her go off.

"You are crazy! Crazy! It is not a problem. Not a problem in Italy." Angelo waves his hands up and down.

"I would like another car. We are not leaving here without another car."

"Lady, there is not another automatic car. We do not drive these cars in Italy."

"Well, if we wreck because we cannot see in the dark, you are liable. We are not!"

After an hour of back and forth with Angelo, nothing has changed. The light is still broken. I grab the keys and get behind the wheel.

"Jackie. Get in this car. We are going *now*. Angelo, it is okay. Hey Angelo, can I have a smoke?" I light up a smoke in the car.

"You are not on the lease. You can't drive the car." She warns.

"Get in the fucking car. *Pronto!*"

And we are off to Todi.

* * *

Todi

After many missed turns and a number of heated arguments, we arrive at the lovely (and free, by the way, which someone is failing to appreciate) townhouse of my friend Daniel. He is a wildly successful New York City lawyer, and incredibly generous and kind. He gave us the house as a present for my 40th birthday. He said he wanted me to experience all that is wonderful about Umbria.

Admittedly, it's pretty medieval in this house. No AC, a washer but no dryer (and she immediately wants to do laundry), and water that needs to be turned on from the outside for an hour before it will run. I turn on the water in the "Aqua" box outside. It doesn't work. I give up. There will be no showers. I will later learn that I turned on the neighbor Mariella's water instead of ours. Oops.

"Listen, I need a drink. And I need to eat. I'm starving. I'm going into town. You can come with me or not. " I say.

We clearly have a lot of leftover car hostility.

I tie my greasy hair up in a tight ponytail. My face is oily, and I need to shave my legs, but there is no water, and I honestly don't care anymore. I don't put on a stitch makeup. I do not even change my clothes. I just really need a cocktail.

Jackie is agreeable. One thing about Jackie—she can drink. This is the *one* thing I will embrace about her each and every single day. I note this in my journal.

We lock the big Medieval door and turn left climbing a steep and narrow cobblestone hill with small merchants' shops on both sides of it—a pizzeria, a café, a dressmaker, a silk scarf maker. I peer in at shops with beautiful squares of pizza laced with zucchini and porcini mushrooms, old men with spectacles, no socks and camel leather loafers sitting in the alley on fold-up chairs playing cards.

I rush into the dressmaker's shop and touch reams of fabric in vibrant colors like sky blue, jade and petal pink. I hold handmade lemon yellow linen napkins.

"I would so love to do know how to do what you do. To make dresses." I approach the owner.

"You could do it. It's not difficult." She shakes her head and smiles.

I doubt I could ever do it, but I start to think of things that I "could" do with my hands. Things that might be simpler but actually fulfill me. Maybe I could move to Italy and acquire a trade and pitch my barely used law degree.

As I exit the dress shop, I look around—everyone seems so old here. Daniel warned about me about the aging population of Todi. He suggested I get the F out of the way in Rome.

Jackie suggests we go to *Pan e Vino*, a restaurant that Daniel recommended in his makeshift guidebook of Todi. However, as we descend down a big hill approaching the restaurant, I spot this tiny charming wine bar directly across the street from it. I peer in. There are large, open and square white glossy magazines and antique books scattered everywhere on chocolate brown wooden picnic tables. The tables are surrounded by white recessed bookshelves stocked

31

with bottles and bottles of red wine with Italian labels I cannot read. There are only a few wooden tables in the place, and small bar area where one lady pours wine and serves pasta. No one is in there. But for some reason, I feel this is the place to go.

It is really amazing in life how everything can turn on one small decision. One path taken, and another not.

If I had just gone into *Pan e Vino*, I wouldn't be telling this story.

So. Here it all begins.

Chapter Four

"Let's go in here. One glass of red. It looks very cool."
I guide Jackie into Enoteca Barilo.

"Okay," she replies. Finally. Agreement.

One glass of red rapidly turns into three. Jackie
and I bond. We discuss my career, her career and her
need to get a new job (she has been laid off and is
currently living off a big severance package). I try to
coach her in work; she coaches me in love.

"I know you have enjoyed your time off, but you
have to go back to work. I know you are nervous, but
you did so well at Colgate. You'll do great in your
new job, too."

"I know but I only want to work for NBC. It's
really the only job I want, and they are on a hiring
freeze." Jackie sips her wine and remains as always,
intransigent.

"Okay, but they *aren't* hiring. You have to look at
other options. What about Miramax? Or HBO? You
love L.A."

"I'm not moving to L.A."

"Okay." I give up. There is no helping her.

"I'm getting sad again about Henry." I sigh and
belt back the Lambrusco.

33

"Listen, he's a total ass. Control freak. You're always like this—bouncing from one guy to the next. You never look at anyone's bad parts."

"I think I've just been unfocused. I don't know what I want. I need to make a list.

That's what my therapist told me to do."

"You know what you want. You've always known what you want. You have just settled and for way less than you are worth. You worked in the freaking Congress for some of the highest profile men ever. You can do anything."

"I don't know about that."

"Listen, it's so true. You are one of the most focused people I know. You'll find the right guy too. *You can have anything you want.*"

We say something about Washington, D.C. or New York City. And suddenly, we are overheard by some locals.

Two men, one table over closer to the open door, who have recently arrived, turn and look over at us.

"Hello. Are you from the States? I heard you say you were. Why don't you come over here and sit with us?"

The older one, middle-aged wild black curls with acne cheek scars and a paunched belly (approximately 48?) shouts over to us.

I immediately rise—red glass elevated in hand. I am excited. Embrace the locals. Adventure! Jackie follows me to their table.

"What are you ladies drinking?" The older one asks as we sit down in the chairs directly across from them.

"It is... it is ... this!" Jackie points to number 13 on the menu.

"No, no. No." The younger one shakes his head. "Let me order." He scans the menu with his index finger. "Let's have this one... the Brunello di Montalcino. And new glasses please."

They speak English well. I'm impressed. I didn't expect this.

I stare at the younger one. He has a round baby face. I am thinking he is like 25. I look away. I feel like a hyena (worse than a cougar actually).

I am almost 40. No makeup on, no concealer to hide the purple bags and not a piece of jewelry. Worn out pale blue Patagonia shorts, distressed brown tee and overworn New Balance tennis shoes. I look like a lesbian.

I can't stop looking at him as I sip each ounce of my wine. I am trying hard to drink slowly like they do. I engage and then disengage. But I notice he keeps looking at me every time I peek up from my wine glass. Or am I imagining this? He swirls his wine from its stem staring down at the wide rimmed glass, and then he looks up from it and directly into my eyes.

I feel nervous and confused. I keep trying to sip the wine, but it's going down so rapidly.

"I'll be back in a minute."

I excuse myself. I need a smoke. I need some air.

I walk down the street and enter a small park overlooking the countryside. I am pacing, but I try to calm down—light a cigarette and look at the recessed green hills and villas buried in deep them and just gaze at the beauty of it all.

Then, I feel someone touch the back of my right shoulder. Abruptly, I turn around. It is him.

"Hello. I do not smoke..." He says.

He reaches for his front jeans' pocket. Pulls out an old-fashioned silver lighter.

"Neither do I. But I am here. It is my week of smoking, and…"

He stops me.

"But I'd like to join you. To take a cigar."

He lights my cigarette slowly and then his cigar. He is moving so very slowly. He is brown but not so Italian brown just a hint of golden brown. He has a cherub face, wide brown-black saucer eyes, a little bit of scruff on the chin. Preppy yet edgy—an untucked, cobalt blue gingham shirt and dark blue tailored jeans, no socks, navy penny loafers. His hair is curly jet black and a bit greasy. He rubs his fingers through it over and over again pushing it from his glossy forehead to the back of his head.

He pulls my arm—pulling me to the small tall wooden table with two chairs right outside the restaurant. I immediately stand up and shift back and forth a bit on my heels and toes and pull at my hair nervously.

But I can't seem to stand still. There is just something. Pulling me toward him like a magnet. I can't stop looking at him. Yet, I can't imagine I am seeing this situation right. I really look like utter hell, and I am so incredibly tired. Is this really happening? How could he possibly be interested in me?

He grabs the very top of my right wrist, pulling me into his chair, and kisses my fingers. "You are so beautiful. You are so, so beautiful. What is your name? "

I stare back at him. Saying and doing nothing.

"What is your name?" He whispers it again pronouncing each syllable.

36

"Esme."

"Esme… that is a beautiful name."

"Thank you." I smile.

"I am Fernando."

He extends his hand, and I take it feeling a jolt surge through my body.

"Hello." I smile again.

I have no idea what to say. I can't even believe this is happening.

"I love your eyes. Your blue eyes." Wow. At least *he* got the color right. The last two men I dated thought they were green.

He takes the cigarette out of my hand and stomps it out with his loafer.

"So tell me… do you have a boyfriend?"

"No."

"No boyfriend?"

"No. No boyfriend." I confirm.

"How could that be? Why do you not have a boyfriend?"

"I had a boyfriend. We broke up. recently."

"Why? Why did you break up?"

"Well, I do not know how you say it in Italian. He was just so… so regimented. Controlling, you know? Everything had to be his way. And I just couldn't deal with it. I don't know. He was selfish. I don't know how to explain it."

"I know. I know. I know what you mean."

"You do?"

"Si, si, I had a girlfriend, the same way. Too many rules. Way too many rules. It is just not… possible."

"Si, si! Exactly. Not possible."

37

And suddenly there, he pulls my chin into his and kisses me deeply. It doesn't stop. It keeps going. Long. Very long.

"I want to taste your lips. I want to taste your tongue." He whispers in my ear. He presses his tongue slowly into my mouth, and I can taste the remnants of the Cuban cigar on it.

I think a thousand things. He is a player. He is an operator. He is a liar. He is a total jerk. He is just trying to get me into bed. I know all of which are likely true. But I don't care. I don't give a flying fuck what lines he has practiced. He is what I want and need right now.

He is the F.

I can't stop. I can't stop looking at him. I can't stop holding his large calloused hands in mine. I think he must be a carpenter. I can't seem to move my body back into my chair. And he is holding on to my upper rib cage bones so tightly as he pulls my body between his legs sprawled open on the stool.

I finally manage to pull away.

"We should go back." I look at him. "Jackie is waiting for me."

I know I need to go back inside.

As we pull away and approach the open door, I feel Jackie's glare. She has seen us kissing. Fuck. She is not happy. I can tell. But then, no one ever approves of my behavior.

"Come with us. Let's go have an after-dinner drink. You like Grappa? Sambuca?" Fernando grabs my wrist looking at me inquisitively. The wrist pulses fervently. The wrist follows.

"No, no." I push him away. "I can't drink that stuff."

"Then perhaps a vodka? Or a champagne?"

"Well, I could do one champagne."

But Jackie has already torn up the steep cobblestone hill. She wants to go home, and she is pissed off at me.

"Just give me the keys! I am exhausted. I just want to go home!"

She turns around as I tear up such hill in my crumbling running shoes.

That bitch.

"Jackie, relax. We're just going to go have one more drink with them. No big deal."

I am out of fucking breath from the smokes.

"I don't want to go. I want to go home! Just give me the keys."

"No! I'm not letting you walk home alone. Good God, we're wasted. And I'm not letting you walk home by yourself. I mean, we don't even know this town!"

We fight. Keys are dropped. Keys are picked up.

Eventually, she capitulates (as she should). We *are* in fucking Italy.

We go to the next place. We drink something. I think a vodka. I can't remember. He is kissing me and rubbing my back. And then stroking my butt under the back of my shorts. This I remember.

Allora!

This is Italy!

Chapter Five

Day Two

The next day, Jackie and I both rise late, very late. I am amazed that after consuming barbaric amounts of liquor, I am not hung over. After a few days of hardcore drinking in Italy, I feel refreshed. I'm used to the drinking now.

I scurry out to get a cappuccino, as I fear the wrath of Jackie. I just know she is going to rip my head off for everything that occurred last night including but not limited to: leaving her, making out with Fernando, forcing her to go out for an after dinner drink. I'm sure I'm forgetting some other things.

I notice in my cell phone a new contact.

"Fernando, Italy guy" programmed in. I laugh. Whatever.

I don't think I'll ever hear from him again although apparently we have exchanged numbers. I don't remember that either.

I go to the local café. Standing up, I swig back a cappuccino in unbridled more-is-better American style. I order another. The men next to me are in black tailored pinstriped suits and dark rose striped ties, talking, hands moving effusively. Some are smoking cigarettes. Others are reading newspapers.

I grab a café to go (which you can't really do in Italy) as a small token of kindness toward Jackie who I know I have royally pissed off. I carry the Dixie cup carefully and steadily as I climb the brick road back to our house.

When I open the door, I hear Jackie talking in a loud voice to someone. As I climb the winding brick stairs to the living room, there is Jackie sitting with Fabio in our living room.

WTF?

I guess she needed a "Vodafone" (Query: Who do you need to call in Europe? It's like 50 fucking cents a minute anyway. Good God). And Fabio, in gentleman-like Italian fashion, picked her up and took her to the freaking AT&T store 15 miles away. And now she has a "TIM card" enabling her phone to work. Thank God. I am so sick of hearing about her not having a phone or wireless here. Who in the hell do you want to talk to anyway? I am desperately trying to avoid my boss, my parents, anyone else who typically pulls at me each and every day.

I hand Jackie the coffee and go upstairs to grab my purse. Will let the potential lovebirds nest.

"I'm taking Daniel's guidebook and going out for a bit."

I holler as I tear down the stairs.

I'm getting hungry. I'm always hungry in Italy. I'm turning into that fucking Liz Gilbert.

I decide to go for some protein. Good for belly flattening, right? At least I won't get fat.

Must continue low food/high alcohol plan.

Daniel's book recommends a *porchetta* (pork) buggy located directly under the Roman arch entering the city. He contends that his neighbor, Enricho, serves sliced pork hot and fresh right off the slaughtered pig's hide. Excellent. I dig the pig.

And for so long now, I have had to wrangle with my penchant for the pig and the subsequent guilt issues it generated.

Arbitrary and Capricious Rule of Henry Number 8: Thou shall not eat pig.

(By the way, he is neither Jewish nor a vegetarian.)

Ironically, I learn about Rule Number 8 while we are in New York City at a restaurant that I picked called, "The Spotted Pig."

We are at brunch. He orders a veggie frittata. I order a huge Cuban sandwich overflowing with pork and onions and cheese.

"You can have some of this." I pick up my sandwich and break it in half. "This is huge!"

"I don't eat pig." He states flatly. Confidently.

"What?" I turn my head to the left and squint. He, like me, is from the Midwest. We eat bacon. We eat pulled pork. We have ham at every holiday.

"What are you talking about?"

"I'm opposed to eating pigs. For ethical reasons."

"What ethical reasons?" I mean, I've seen him eat plenty of chicken and turkey. I bite into my sandwich. So salty and juicy. I wipe off the juice splattered over my cheek. So dig the pig. What the fuck is wrong with him?

"Pigs are intelligent animals, Esme. I learned about this in med school. They are highly intelligent

42

animals—more so even than dogs. They can *feel*, Esme. They can *think*."

There is always that distinct enunciation of the two syllables of my name, which annoys me.

"You don't eat pig? For ethical reasons? But you will eat birds... birds that are not in free-range settings most of the time and are slaughtered brutally?"

"I am not going to eat a pig. I never wanted to dissect one. They are very intelligent, and it is wrong to eat pigs."

"Not even bacon? How could you not eat bacon?"

"I haven't had a slice of bacon in nine years."

And this is a rule. And it's a stupid one. It is a pig for Christsakes, and if you are going to pull some sanctimonious vegetarianism on me, be consistent. No animals. No dairy. That is the message, Henry. Birds do not trump pigs.

And that is that. Because! *That is Rule Number 8. No pigs.*

I never stopped eating pig. But I stopped eating it in front of Henry because I always felt I was being judged for my penchant for the hooves.

But gazing down now upon a Medieval brick courtyard framed with flowers, free from the rules and judgments that I have left behind me, I am going to celebrate my freedom by ripping open this inhumanely slaughtered pig. I'm going to chow it down without a nanosecond of regret.

As I'm wiping off my pig-juice lips, my phone beeps. A text message.

It is "Fernando, Italy guy."

"*Boun giorno*, bella. How are you?"

I lean back. My eyes pop.

"Great. How r u?" I text back fervently.

Finally, things are getting good. It's about fucking time.

"I'm good."

I pause.

"Today I would like to take you to a waterfall. The most beautiful in all of Europe. If you prefer."

"OK. OK." I text back

"Pick you up @ 3?"

"C u then."

I rush home and dart up the stairs. Jackie and Fabio are seated calmly on the living room sofa exploring the Vodaphone.

I skid around the kitchen table, pushing the vegetable cart to the side. I take her beloved phone out of her hands and grab her shoulders and shake her.

"Jackie, listen. Fernando called! He wants to take us to this waterfall. The tallest waterfall in all of Europe! He is coming at three. Get in the shower. Let's go!"

"No. I'm not going."

She declines in a calm measured voice and grabs the phone from my hands and starts pushing its buttons.

"I'm exhausted. You kept me out late. Then the fucking pigeons cooed all night, and then the rooster woke me up. And it was so hot up there. I don't think I slept all night."

"Jackie, come on. Get a shower. You must go. The waterfall in Terni—it's magnificent. You must go," Fabio coaxes her.

"Come on, Jackie." I pull her hands off the sofa. "*Carpe diem*! We are in Italy for God sakes. We can sleep when we are dead."

44

"I am not going. I am *not* going." She states adamantly.

"I'll get you an espresso. Please! Let's rally!" I plea.

"No. No. I'm not going." She gets up and walks toward the staircase. "I need a nap. And by the way, I'm not driving the car. And I'm not hanging out with these guys all week."

She pulls me aside in the kitchen. I open up the fridge and grab a beer.

Finally, I let it go. She can fucking sleep. I'm out of here!

Fernando arrives. Late. Very late. And I *hate* late.

I am wearing a simple white sundress purchased days ago in a Rome boutique and white flip-flops. I hear Fernando's car pull up the street, and I walk up the stone path to meet him. He approaches me in a navy blue mesh Izod polo, dark blue jeans rolled up at the bottom and chocolate Ferragamo loafers. RayBan Wayfarers and an oversized Rolex watch. My heart starts to race.

I cannot take my eyes off of him.

"Ciao bella."

He kisses each of my cheeks.

I do the same even though I am Midwestern and reserved by nature (I eschew hugs let alone kisses). I feel awkward. I am sure I am tripping over myself, and my neck is stiff.

"You smell very good. What perfume are you wearing?"

"You are very late."

I will never get used to be people being late. I have always felt it conveys, in a passive-aggressive manner, two messages: i.) I am more important than you are, and ii.) your time is not as valuable as mine.

He looks at his oversized silver watch.

"Si, si. I'm sorry." He sighs. "I had to get gas. It's… it's complicated."

"I do not like late."

"Si, si, captain. I understand. But Italians… we move *slowly*." He laughs.

This is something I will soon get very used to.

"Shall we go?" He kisses my hand.

"Yes."

"Is Jackie coming?"

"No, she is going to rest."

"Rest?!" He is shocked.

"Yes, she is very tired. Fabio is coming though."

"Good. Good."

He states calmly in his soft breathy high-pitched voice. He is laidback and at peace in the world. He needs to drain a vial of his blood and give some of it to Jackie to drink. I also can't believe how easy it is to communicate with him. He speaks English so well.

"How come you speak English so well? Did you learn it in school?"

"No. no. I studied it a little bit at university, but not too much."

"Then, how do you know English so well?"

"American movies and music and television, darling," he grabs my hand and smiles.

"I taught myself. I just listened." He states.

My heart melts. A curious mind. A self taught and motivated man. Wow.

We get into his silver Golf VW and drive for miles and miles over yellow countryside roads. He puts in a CD, an homage to Fellini by Caetano Veloso. It is simply beautiful. I turn it up. The violins are full of sadness and regret, and the cello is pronounced and heavy, but the music is exhilarating as it evaporates into the country air.

"Who is this?" I ask him as I flip the CD in my hands.

"It is Veloso. A Brazilian singer. You know the filmmaker Fellini?"

"Yes, of course. *La Dolce Vita!*" I smile.

"Yes. Yes." He smiles. "This is a tribute for him."

"It's beautiful." I smile. He holds my hand and kisses it, over and over.

"Si, bellissima."

He slips on his sunglasses. I melt into the hot leather seat next to him.

We jam to Led Zeppelin. Then Pink Floyd.

Fabio sings in the back pounding his fists on my seat, and Fernando sings loudly, "Run, run, run! " Tapping his fingers on the wheel.

I sit in the front leafing through scattered magazines that are draped on the floor of the car. They are *GQ, Details,* and an oversized magazine with picture after picture of luxury cars. I open it and leaf through the pages.

"Aston Martin?" What is this?"

"Ohhh!" they sigh simultaneously. "We love Ashton Martin!"

"Are you kidding me?''

"Si, si, you do not like?" Fernando looks at me inquisitively.

"No, no, not in the U.S.... Quattro formaggi! (four cheeses)."

They laugh.

"Cheesy?" Fabio turns to me.

"Yes! Yes! Totally cheesy!"

"Well, I will have one… one day… when I live in America!" James Bond… Giacomo Bondi! He had one." Fernando exclaims.

I roll my eyes.

"We love James Bond! And The Godfather!"

"Blah! So 1972!" I counter.

As we pass the open countryside, yellow sunflowers with long necks and black eyes arch in different directions toward the sun, white cotton clouds barely moving, rooftop off the car. Driving fast through windy roads with no guardrail. I feel like we could go over the cliff at any moment, but I am not scared.

I tell myself to savor this moment.

I mean, really savor it. I am high. Truly high. I want this moment to last forever. I do not want it to ever end. I want to bottle it up. I promise myself that when I get home, I really am going to start living in the moment instead of worrying about every possible thing that could go wrong next week.

We drive and drive down many curved passages, and suddenly we are going down a long, winding unpaved road that leads into a dense deep forest.

I start to panic... just a bit.

"Where are we going, Fernando?"

He laughs.

"You know last night, you called me Bernardo. Then Bernando. Never Fernando. I am just happy you remembered my name."

"I know, I know. Jackie told me that this

morning. What can I say? I was wasted. I'm sorry. I know your name now."

"Good. Remember it." He looks over at me and kisses the tips of my fingers.

He parks the car in the middle of fucking nowhere on top of some crumbled stones. I cannot see any waterfall. I only see tall trees in a vast forest and no humans. I know we are now near the city of Terni but not much else. I keep thinking, *Fuck, if I get raped by these guys, or fall and break my ankle, what will I do?*

I mean, I have my iPhone, but what will I text Daniel? Send a helicopter rescue? I am somewhere in the woods near this town called Terni, near a big waterfall. I already envision myself crawling up rocks and twigs with bloody knees, bruised, with no sense of direction. And Jackie isn't even with me. Fuck.

My heart is racing. I barely know these guys. In fact, I don't know them at all. Maybe I have taken my purported sense of adventure too far this time. If I get killed, no one would ever find me. My poor parents. Clawing at my empty coffin, filled with regret because they were the ones who told me to go to Italy and take a vacation... my know-it-all younger sister shaking her head, purportedly in grief, telling my parents she told them so, that I've always been crazy and too trusting of strangers. My steadfast physician brother who has never even left the U.S., lamenting that once again his out-of-control sister's sense of adventure and failure to abide by conventional social norms resulted in her bloody tragic death that anyone who knew me could have predicted...

"You guys..."

I step out of the car, vacillating.

"I'm kind of nervous. I mean, this kind of looks

like the place a serial killer would take his next victim," I whisper.

Fabio laughs—kind of.

"I know. I know." He says. " You probably think we are murderers, but we're actually really nice guys. *We are gentlemen.*"

He is overweight and breathing heavily, wiping the sweat off his acne-scarred face.

"Do not worry. It is okay. This is a path only Italians know," Fernando whispers.

He takes my hand into his wide palm and guides me down a descending dirt path into the forest. Okay, there is a fine line between "adventure" and "risk," and at this point, I think I have migrated into the risk category. I have my purse. I hold my phone tightly. I still envision myself climbing up rocks, bloody and disheveled, texting Daniel (who is in constant communication with us from the U.S. in between his myriad client meetings) or worse yet, to Jackie, me explaining:

- Where I am for purposes of the emergency rescue by the rudimentary Italian helicopter which may or may not make it.
- How I managed to get myself raped and stabbed in the woods.
- Why I didn't just stay back with Jackie and take a nap as any normal American tourist would have done.

My heart is racing, and sweat is pouring down my forehead and through my bra. That's the thing about an adventure—it wouldn't be one if you weren't at least a little bit scared.

But, after about 30 steps and 50 large jagged stones, I look into his eyes, and I feel okay.

"Come on. Come, it's okay."

He holds my hand more tightly, and pulls me slowly down the terrain.

"Go *slowly*. Watch your step. Come on, now. "

And I feel safe. For once, I trust my instincts. I don't believe anymore that they are going to rape and kill me. I see something warm and safe and peaceful in his eyes.

Fernando starts to walk a bit ahead of me, but as he skips a stone or two, he stops and reaches for my hand guiding me every step of the way. I slip on loose rocks. He catches me every time.

We laugh hysterically. Fabio is inappropriately dressed in khakis and loafers, sweating profusely and huffing and puffing. I am barely making it in flip flops, sweating as well, feeling like at any moment I'm going to wipe out and break my ankle.

"Fernando! Fernando! What the fuck? How much longer? What were you thinking? Jesus." Fabio exclaims.

Fernando laughs and laughs.

"Look at Fabio. He needs to go the gym."

"Stop! I need a rest." Fabio says.

Fabio pauses as we are about halfway down the trail. He sits on a big boulder and has a smoke.

I am laughing uncontrollably. This is an insane endeavor on so many levels, but guess what? We are doing it.

After 458 steps (Fabio has counted each of them), we arrive.

"See? See?" Fernando grabs my hand at the bottom of the trail. "Isn't it amazing?" He presses me against a guardrail on top of the cliff, and wraps his arms tightly around my waist. "So beautiful, no?"

And it is.

One tall waterfall with two smaller sister falls next to it cascading down in many white streams into a pine-green lake emanating circles and circles of placid waves. It is the tallest, purest waterfall I have ever seen. I could stare at the water forever, and we really do have the absolute best view in the world. And it is a view no one knows about but us.

I am a materialistic girl. I typically look only at handbags and shoes and the fabric of dresses. But I can't help but relish the waterfall. Allora! It is pristine and the air is open and pure, and the falling of water never stops. And as he pulls me closer to him, I can't help but think that this one of the best views I have ever had. I etch it all deep into my mind. I vow to write about it in my journal tonight.

We pose. Arms wide open. We take photos. We laugh.

I reach my hand over the balcony almost falling and grab the guardrail to balance myself. I stretch my hand—bending my waist over the rail and into the water. I run my hands in the water, and bring to my mouth and taste it. It is cool and refreshing and pure. I reach for it again as Fernando holds my thighs firmly against the rail.

"Hey… hey… wait. He laughs. "You are going to fall into the water! Be careful."

"It's amazing!" I splash the cool invigorating water all over my face.

He wipes my face with his shirt and laughs.

"I told you… it's amazing, no?"

"It is amazing!" I kiss him on the lips. "I'm so glad we came."

"I knew you would like it. I want you to experience *everything* here in Italy."

Now, though, it is time to go back. And I have no idea how we're going to get back up that long hill.

Finally, we begin. Slower and more measured this time. More cautiously. I pass them both. Despite all the recent smoking, I am a trained runner and solid hiker. I can do this rapidly even in a snug dress. They move *slowly*. For them, there is no rush. What am I sprinting for? I have nowhere to be.

About a quarter way back up the hill, Fabio stops.

"I need a rest. I need to stop."

We stop. I grab tissue from my purse, and we wipe off our faces. Fernando rubs his on my forehead first. Fabio lights up a cigar.

"Come on! Come on!" I motion them both upward. "Let's go!" I move fast, always.

"Relax, bella. There is no hurry. Italians *move slowly.*"

I'm starting to get it.

But then. I'm also very done with nature. Especially in a white fucking sundress.

We finally summit. The top of the hill.

"What would you like? What would you like to do next?" Fernando asks me as we approach the car.

"I need a drink."

"Yes. Yes, *signora*. Let's get a beer and some water. Is that good with you?"

"Yes, yes. *Perfetto*! I really need a beer."

I haven't had a drink in hours. My hands are starting to shake.

We jump in the car and jam to Nirvana, passing ivory waterfalls and verdant hills and haystacks, tightly wound like spools of thread, in vast copper fields. Fernando sings loudly and looks over at me. I just hold his hand and laugh.

As I look out on the beautiful landscape, I tell myself over and over, *I will not want. I will not sweat the small stuff. I won't take work so seriously when I get back.* This is what life is about—this moment, this experience.

We go to a dark pub with only a few wooden picnic tables. It is a place they know well, and the young waitress kisses his cheeks as we walk in. I feel this small ping of jealousy. How does he know her? Did they ever date? Is she sleeping with him? Ridiculous thoughts… what am I thinking?

"What would you like to eat, darling? You must be hungry."

He hands me the menu which I cannot read.

"I'm starving. I don't know…. Maybe….."

"We'll take an *aperitif.* How about some salami, prosciutto, a little cheese, olives? Sound good? Si?"

"Yes. That sounds perfect."

"*Bouno*! Let's do it." He slams the menu down on the table.

He seems to know what I need and what I want even before I do. I am hungry, and he knows exactly what I want to eat. I am thirsty, and the coldest best tasting beer ever arrives. When I thought I was going to fall on the rocks during the hike, he was right there to catch me. I can't remember ever feeling this "attended to." It is like his whole role on this planet is to make sure I have everything I want. I feel high, exuberant, exhilarated.

"You did well, back there." He says.

He strokes my arm. My veins pulse. Even the smallest touch by him sends electric shocks through my body.

"Thanks, well, I almost wiped out ... many times."

"You are in good shape. You have very muscular legs."

"I'm a runner."

"You're a runner?" He seems stunned or pleased. I can't tell which.

"Yes, I actually run when I am not smoking." I smile and light up a cigarette. "*Si, si*, I'm a runner too. We have to go running *together*. There is a beautiful park here in Terni, right near my apartment. We will go there together."

Yes! Another common interest. Another activity we can do together. We are so compatible.

"Yes. Let's go running." I reach for his hand.

"Do you do races? Marathons?"

"Yes. I have done a couple marathons... but it was awhile ago."

"*Si, si.* I'm doing a marathon in China in November. Allesandro said he would do it with me, but I doubt he will. Why don't you do it with me?"

"In China?"

"*Si*, it's in the mountains, but we have time to train."

"Okay, let's do it!"

Suddenly, globetrotting all over the world even to China to do a marathon seems perfectly reasonable and within reach. Why not? We are jetsetters. I can get another week off work. I can go to China. I can pull 26

55

miles together in three months. With him, I feel that *anything is possible.*

We order another beer and then another. I eat the salami and the Parma and then olives. The food is incredible and the beer is bold and slightly bitter. I know we will have dinner soon, but I can't stop. Every nerve in my body is heightened. The clanging of high heels on the street seem louder, and the green bottles of beer seem greener, bolder, vibrant. My head spins. I pray he doesn't leave me midweek. I need this man.

Chapter Six

When we get back to house later that day, Jackie is not in better spirits. Her nap was not as fruitful as expected. Her Ambien did not work. The rooster was crowing again. There were the pigeons flocking outside the windows. The house doesn't have air conditioning, and she is hot.

"Jackie, that waterfall was amazing. Fucking amazing. I *cannot* believe you missed it." I am pacing and taking faster and faster. "Truly! It was so fun!"

"I needed to sleep. I couldn't have done it. *You* kept me up last night."

Good lord. Here we go. We were out till two. We are not grandparents.

"Chop. Chop!" I tell her.

We will shower and then go to Fernando's restaurant. He wants to cook a lavish dinner for us. It will be magnificent. (Fernando just happens to be a chef too. How hot is that?)

"Put on a sexy black dress for me," he whispers in my ear as we walk up the stairs of Daniel's house.

I feel obligated to do so now, given my appearance of last night. So I do.

"I will make you a beautiful dinner... *bruschetta*...

some *salade*… a little pasta… some *ricotta*… a *secondi* maybe *branzino.*" He rubs his scruffy chin. "Tiramisu."

I'm salivating like a ravished dog.

But Jackie will not budge.

I make her shower and motivate. I need to get a vino rosso in her as soon as possible.

When we arrive at his small white-roofed restaurant, we sit outside on small white plastic tables draped with red-checkered tablecloths with all his *amicis.* Alessandro the printer, Fabrizio the pizzeria owner, Francesco the baker. They drink and smoke and eat. The Village People, taking a relax.

Fernando brings course after course after course of beautiful food. A bowl of juicy wet *ricotta* you simply pull with your fingers and eat. Buffalo mozzarella, imported from Turin, on top of roma tomatoes drenched in olive oil and fresh basil. Thin slices of pizza with triangle zucchinis and porcini mushrooms. Pasta carbonara.

I think I'm going to explode, but he forces me to eat more.

Query: Am I turning into fucking Liz Gilbert now? Am I really going to *eat*, gain ten pounds, and completely ruin my fucking story?

At dinner, he sits next to me, pulling me closer to him and kissing my cheek. He slides my chair toward his.

"*Vicini, vicini,*" he keeps whispering in my ear.

"What does that mean?"

"Near. Near." He says slowly. "Come near." He pulls my chair closer to his.

"You are so beautiful. So *very* beautiful." He kisses my neck up and down.

I know. I know. It sounds like I'm desperate for male attention. I get that. This really is a bit too gushy, even for me. I really do not like public displays of affection. I do not like the nice guys. They tend to bore me. Or want me to meet their parents.

But I haven't heard words like that in a very long time. So cut me a break here.

"I want you to stay with me tonight, if you prefer." He kisses the top of my ear and the artery below it on my neck.

I ignore it. *Come on.* It's way, way too soon.

Later, he says it again.

"I want you to stay. Please. Stay with me tonight. If you prefer."

Then, I think. I think of the story. Here's the thing. I know I am going to fuck him sooner or later, right?

I pause. Think some more. Drink some more. The decision rapidly becomes easier to make.

Fuck it. I have only one week. Best to maximize this. Time is limited. Every single day counts. I want this party started right now.

I agree to stay with him. Jackie is pissed as hell, but Fabio drives her back to Todi. She can deal. I mean, I already told her at the airport that I was going to smoke, drink and fuck. *She knew all this.*

"Darling, do you want some champagne? We should drink champagne at my house." He pulls my hand into his as we leave the restaurant and walk down the dark streets.

"Si. Si." I nod. Why the hell not? I love champagne. And it is pretty romantic, you must admit. We get pink champagne to go at a local bar.

I enter his old but modernly decorated U-shaped apartment. It is quite big (by DC standards), and it has beautiful but dark, somewhat disturbing artwork on the walls. A woman screaming in a red-and-black dress over his sofa. Black and white photos of starving children in his kitchen on tall, stark white walls. There are black and white oak-framed photos of his family next to the TV. His mother young, before she died a few years ago, with long black hair that is blowing at the sea. One of his father, who has his build and his dimpled chin, painting at his studio. There is Salinger's *Nine Stories* on the oval dining room table.

"You really do read Salinger?" I ask him picking up the book.

"Yes."

"Salinger." I hug the book.

I pull Paul Auster's *Leviathan*, off the bookshelf, and D.H. Lawrence's *Women in Love.*

"I love, love Paul Auster. Have you read this book?" I open it up.

"Yes. Yes. I told you. I love American Lit-tor-ture," he states.

"Really?"

"Yes, yes. I studied it a bit at university. Philip Roth, he is my favorite." He pulls *Portnoy's Complaint* off the shelf.

Now that is *hot,* no? I mean what *American* man reads Paul Auster? Maybe Philip Roth because he is so perverted. But please.

I mean, please.

He pops open the champagne. It is pink and bubbly and warm. It mirrors my exact mood right now. He pulls me by my elbow down the hall into his bedroom.

He pours the champagne into two elegant flutes. We chug it. I cannot even tell you how many how drinks or smokes I have had it at this point. But who cares? I do think it is now time for next part of the story.

Allora!

He grabs my chin and looks penetratingly into my eyes. Wow. This is so intense.

"Si, *tu es bellissima*! You are so so beautiful."

I turn away. I start to feel overwhelmed and want to retreat.

He grabs my chin and pulls me back.

"You are so, so beautiful. You have the most beautiful eyes." He kisses my eyelids.

Again, I know: *Quattro Formaggi*. But I did just get out of a relationship with a man, who told me after I showered and shaved and primped to the highest degree, that "I cleaned up nice." There was no beautiful. There was not even a pretty.

He pulls up my black sheer dress and pushes me onto the white linen bed. He tears off my underwear as I awkwardly unbutton his Venetian jeans. He unfastens my strapless bra and rubs his tongue against my nipples, working himself down to my navel and then on the bones of my pelvis, against my inner thighs. He keeps going between my legs and pushes me back. When I cannot come (for reasons still unclear to me), I tell him he should stop now, but he doesn't stop. He pushes my hands down firmly onto the white sheets and holds them there. His lips and tongue move deep inside me, and as he gets to the right spot, I push him away. He whispers:

"I would like to continue." And he does.

I lay back and try to just relax. My stomach tightens, and my legs collapse with ease and without effort.

"You taste wonderful. So sweet. So sweet." His mouth moves in circles, and then his tongue penetrates me forcefully.

I groan, and I pant. I can't breath.

"Oh my God. Oh my God." He stops.

"You're driving me crazy." I gasp.

"I love doing this to you. I could do this all day."

"Why?"

"It makes me feel close to you. I want to be close to you."

I lose myself in it and in him. My inner thighs quake. I can't stop it and know I am so close. I sigh with relief and with deep pleasure that I never thought I would find. He is man that actually cares about what I feel... what I need.

Come on girls: What American man ever says that to you? I couldn't even get the Robot to go downtown.

Allora!

And for the first time in my life, I am not neurotic. I am not worried about a possible cellulite spotting. I am not worried if I am thin enough or if I am perfectly waxed. I'm not looking at my stomach to see if it is flat or if my legs are perfectly shaved. I am perfectly comfortable in my own skin and at one with my body with all of its warts and imperfections. I move around, indifferent to everything.

We do it over and over—I would guess, four times in one night (to be fair, that does include the morning). These youngsters. They can really perform.

They are up. They are down. And then they are up again. Good Gawd.

Note to self: I am now officially *over* the 40- and 50-somethings I have been dating for far too long—the "I can't get it up / if I can get it up I can't keep it up for more than ten minutes" guys.

Fuck that noise.

I would say I couldn't keep up with him, but then, I've always had a lot of energy. It seriously is the most amazing sex that I've ever had. Well, I guess I cannot say "ever" because I honestly can't remember all my lovers at this point. But, it is at least the most amazing sex I have had in the last decade.

Note to reader: The Italians are *amazing* lovers. Go Italian, girls. Pronto.

In addition, all night long, there is never one moment when we are not embracing each other in some way. He is always holding my hand, touching my shoulder, draping his arm around my stomach, or moving over to whatever spot in the bed where I am located. We are *vicini vicini*, as he told me earlier—he only had a bed for one and a half. I feel constantly and incessantly adored. I feel safe. It is an amazing, previously before unfelt feeling. I finally feel like I fit into the body of someone else, like the one missing piece of a 100-piece puzzle that I have been searching for.

In the morning, we lay there in the heat and the sweat and bright white sun with a slight warm breeze emanating through the tall white half-open wooden shutters that are clapping from the summer breeze. We laugh as the church bells ring every hour. My hair and neck are damp. I have never felt so gross, and I never felt so good at gross. He reaches over and grabs my hand, placing it on his heart. He passes me the tall bottle of mineral water from last night and murmurs, "Ohhh. You are so beautiful," as he kisses the nape of my neck over and over. I rub my hands over his fingers; his cuticles are ragged and need to be cut. His neck smells of pine. I can't stop smelling his neck. He lies on top of me and kisses me and licks the pools of sweat off my throat, and enters me again. I arch my back and let him. It seems that it will never end. Then we lay there taking deep breaths and disbanding.

He gets up and hands me a plush white robe. He walks slowly and silently toward the bathroom. He is tall and sculptured in Michelangelo's David marble style. I cannot stop staring at his perfectly round ass. I am not one who "stares" at the male body, but as he walks away, I cannot stop looking at him. I could look at him for hours.

"Take a shower. Relax. You can use my toothbrush. Whatever you need." He kisses my forehead and then goes into the bathroom and turns on the shower. He moves quietly into the kitchen and reads the paper.

I shower. I do not wash my hair. I do not shave. I use his toothbrush.

I look my now middle-aged face in the mirror. I don't look old anymore. The crows' feet and purple circles under my eyes have vanished. I look relaxed and dare I say it... happy. I don't even see *me* anymore.

The breakfast with him is still my favorite part of everything.

Because, guess what? I haven't had a breakfast

with a man like this for… well… it must be years. The robot would make me a quick coffee and rush me out of the door as he had a standing 9:00 a.m. tennis appointment likely followed immediately thereafter with gym session. There would be no cuddling. There would be no breakfast. And this was non-negotiable. It was one of his "rules."

When I walk into the cold black-and-white tiled kitchen, wrapped in white terrycloth, hair still dripping, he is sitting there peacefully in an oversized navy blue, gold-crested robe, leafing through the newspaper, boiling water for the stovetop Bialetti espresso maker.

He immediately puts the paper down.

"Buon giorno, bella. Do you want a café?" He walks over to the small white stove where the *Bialetti* sits.

"Yes, please." I slip down into one of the four wooden kitchen chairs surrounding the round pale pine table.

He reaches for the counter and pours espresso into a tiny white demitasse cup. I can't believe how tiny everything is here. The stove is tiny, the refrigerator is the size of my dorm room fridge, and even that coffee pot is no more than 12 inches tall and three inches wide.

And we sit there. And we talk. *Slowly.* About his restaurant. The short story collection on his countertop, and his love of wine and the blog he writes about it. Berlusconi and how his corrupt politics have ruined Italy. His desire to move to the U.S. and open a restaurant with 300 customers not 30 as he has here.

My hair is rapidly turning frizzy curly from poker

straight, but for once, I do not reach for the straightening iron or the Moroccan oil or one of the myriad products I use daily to straighten it. I just *let it go.*

He is the anti-Henry. There are no early morning appointments. He just talks and talks, and there is no rush. And for once, I just listen without anything to say. I don't want him to know me or that I worked for members of Congress or that I am damaged goods from a litany of failed relationships. I just want to be someone else. I will be the person that I want to be— that he wants me to be for just today.

"I will make you some more." He walks over to the stove after I swig back my one shot. Fuck. I need a lot more coffee than this.

"Oh, it's okay." I smile. "I'm fine."

"I have a better idea." He takes my hand into his.

"We will go to breakfast. We will have a pastry or some cookies. And we will take a cappuccino. You like cappuccinos better, no?"

"Yes, I like cappuccinos better."

"Well, we will take breakfast, and we will talk… as long as you like. And when you are done, we will take the train back to Todi. We will stay as long as you like."

"Okay." I smile.

"Che ridi? Che ridi?" He asks pulling my hand into his firmly.

"What does that mean?"

"It means… why are you smiling? Why are you smiling?"

I shake my head. There is no answer.

"I do not know. You make me laugh."

I am happy.

"*You* make me happy, *bella*. I am so glad we met. I'm so glad I met *you.*"

And with that, he pulls down the left shoulder of my white robe and grabs firmly my left breast, pulling me over to him and on top of him, kissing my neck firmly and rapidly up and down, spreading my legs and entering me again. We move, wordlessly and effortlessly, in a cadence that is both natural and familiar.

From the first moment, everything between us felt so natural. Everything. It does, for once, feel effortless and right.

We stay at the table hugging. He is still moaning.

And there really is nothing better than this feeling. Some guy wants to not rush you out the door for his scheduled day of scheduled things. He just wants to hang out, talk, and enjoy the morning... or screw at the kitchen table. This is what I wanted from the last two boyfriends. This is what I have wanted my entire life.

We get dressed. Me in the walk-of-shame black dress/black heels ensemble. But here, there is no judgment. No rules. No one cares about what you did last night. There is always a new day, fresh with opportunity and choices.

We slip into a little bakery in his neighborhood. I eat half a croissant and take a cappuccino. This time I sip it *s l o w l y*. And he talks. I have vowed not to talk. I do not want to talk.

I don't want to talk about Henry, although he has asked me some things about him. He asked me about my job, and I was vague in my response. He doesn't need to know that I worked on Capitol Hill. He doesn't need to know I went to law school or that I write short stories that are published on a national blog. I don't want him to know any of it because I don't want him to know *me*. It isn't important.

And like most men, he is happy to just talk about himself. I listen kind of, but I often check out and look at the glass cabinets full of little cookies. I don't really want to know his story. I just want to drink this amazing coffee and look at him.

At times, we say nothing. Nothing at all. But the silences are not awkward; they are peaceful and welcome.

I listen to the pigeons. I look at the little boys with jet-black pixie haircuts and striped shirts kicking a soccer ball down an alley. I look at the elegant woman next to me sweeping her long black hair to the side and slipping her lilac leather handbag over her shoulder. When my cup is half empty, he gets me another. And then another. As usual, before I speak, he anticipates my every need.

I stare at the passersby—the woman with high heels pushing twins in a robin blue stroller, the elderly woman opening lifting up shades and opening her gelato shop, the pizza guy from last night slapping large pizzas on stones into deep ovens. There is pride here in everything—your appearance, your craft, the food you eat.

Fernando and I sip cafés, then walk to the train station holding hands and not speaking. It seems that we are *always* holding hands, all through Italy. And I, who never touches anyone in public, am somehow embracing it.

WTF?

We slide into the red leather train booth. We laugh out loud at the strange music emanating out of some teenager's mobile phone next to us. I press my head against the window and stare at the bales of hay and the sunflowers. I say nothing.

He talks though. He tells me about his mother and her recent death from breast cancer. His Dutch father, a famous artist, who has disappeared but is likely hiding out in Rotterdam. How he and his best friend, Antonio, plan to go there in December to find him. About his parents' tumultuous marriage and his father's gambling addiction and alcoholism. Again about that marathon he will run in China in November. About his wine blog and his dream of becoming a food and wine critic.

I do not ask questions. I do not offer anything about my life. I will be gone soon. I don't want him to know a thing about me. What's the point? The point is there is no point. I'll be leaving soon and will never see him again. And I don't want to see him again. No more whirlwind romances and getting sucked into it all. It is what it is. Just enjoy it for now.

He rubs my knee and pulls me closer to him. I look at the broken spider vein on it. I make a mental note to get that thing lasered off when I get home. It is one of the things I forgot on my self-improvement kick of last year, but I'm still 39. There is still time to fix this.

"I want you so much now," he whispers in my ear. "You are so handsome."

"Handsome?"

"*Si, si*, handsome."

69

"No! No! Handsome is for men. Pretty is for women."

He laughs.

"Okay, you are so handsome."

"Okay, you are so pretty." I smack his face gently.

"Ummm… I love trains… and being with you on trains," he whispers in my ear.

Now that is what I *want* to hear. I think about "Risky Business." I think about doing it on the train. However, I decide, in a rare moment of rationality, that this is not a prudent course to pursue. I do not want to go to Italian jail. I mean, it is still allegedly, a Catholic nation.

I know I am a sinner. But I figure I'm going to do a lot of bad shit here, and then I'll go repent and get forgiven when I get back home.

Plus, right now, I just want to rest and look out the window.

When we arrive at the Todi train station, I quickly kiss him goodbye on the cheek. I do not ask about later tonight. I do not ask about tomorrow. I do not care.

"I want to see you tonight. I will call you after I work. I have to work some today." He sighs.

"I do not want to say goodbye to you, beautiful girl." He hugs me tightly.

I do not respond. I'm glad he is working. I like industrious men. I was starting to think these Italians never worked. They always seem to be "taking a relax."

I glance at my watch. It's after 11. All I can think about is that I'm very late, and Jackie is going to be pissed off at me. She wanted to go to her rich American friend's villa today.

By the way, in case you are wondering, I am fully aware that I am being a total narcissist now and rude and self-centered. I am not that stupid. But I just can't stop myself. I'm having too much fun.

I do know that she is *always* hungry. I stop at the *drogheria* (grocery store). I pick up a big hunk of *Parma* and somehow manage to finagle an espresso "to go."

When I get home, she is not there.

However, there is a note waiting for me on the kitchen table:

"Ciao bella! It is 11:30 a.m. I waited for you but decided to go to Anna's. Have a good day! I will call you later. Xoxo Jackie"

She knows I would have liked to have gone to the rich American's house and swim. We discussed this possible outing on the plane. Ah. The payback I've been waiting for. Revenge is a dish best served in a cold note.

Fuck. She has the car.

I wanted to go to Todi Rodini Spa (described graphically in Daniel's makeshift guidebook) today and take a relax. Get a massage and facial. Have a glass of wine in the adjacent vineyard.

But I'm stuck at the mothership.

I go to the town square and eat a light salad with rocket and tomatoes, and spaghetti with a hunk of fresh Parma sprinkled all over it. I have three Proseccos. Must keep drinking. Two smokes. I open my yellow leather journal, and take out the blue felt tip pen I always use and scribble notes about the night before in my journal. Then, I'm off.

I watch the streets and the people. I meet Italian

71

cops and take their pictures. I take more notes. I get followed by a mute townie who looks possessed. I'm used to being pursued by freaks, though. I duck into a café and take an espresso. I write some more. I buy a big gold bracelet and some pale pink linen napkins for my Martha Stewart mother who will not appreciate them, forcing me to bring them back to my own new apartment.

I check my texts often, as I am accustomed to doing all day long at work. Nothing. Wow. No one needs me… for anything. At first it's a bit unnerving but only for a second, then it's fucking liberating. I can leave. I can escape without notice. I am can go anywhere. I am *free*.

And finally, his name pops up. Fernando. I have to admit, I was kind of checking for his texts.

"Bouno sera, bella."

"Ciao." I text back.

"Pick you up @ 7. *We will have an aperitif and then some dinner. We will go outside or to an agriturisimo*. Whatever you prefer."

"Si." I text back.

"Have some ideas, but u r the captain, I am your commandante. U pick."

"Good!" I text.

"By the way, what is an *agriturisimo*?

"Like a restaurant on a farm. Fresh tomatoes!"

"Ok! I want to go there."

For once a man is letting me pick where we will eat instead of telling me what we will not be eating. And he will be picking me up instead of asking me to cab or take the subway to some location convenient to him. It's nice to have choices and not be bossed around.

Finally, Jackie texts.

"*Ciao*! Hope ur not mad. @ Anna Maria's house. Amazing! She has a chef! And a pool! U would love it. @ pool now can finally check email!"

Thank fucking God. She has found wireless. I thank the universe. But… she texts me to make sure I'm not angry, yet takes the opportunity to rub my nose in how perfectly delightful the place is and how much I would love it?

"No worries. Enjoy." I light a cig on the patio and text.

"Coming home soon." She texts back.

"OK. Fernando wants to pick us up @ 7 for *aperitif* and dinner." (I will always invite her to each and every outing. I'm not *that* bad of a friend.)

I spend the remainder of the day primping. I take a long, not-so-hot shower and shave (everything) and lather on a pomegranate mask. I straighten every single tress of my long unruly curly hair.

I don't know why I'm doing all this work again for a man who thinks I look beautiful just the way I am… who fell for me the night I wasn't wearing any makeup. I wonder, "Where did the relaxed me go? Am I starting to return to my old neurotic and insecure ways? Am I just overly accustomed to being with men like Henry who require and demand perfection?"

I look at my stomach. I'm starting to look bloated from all the freaking carbs. I wasn't supposed to be eating here—just smoking, drinking and fucking. I start to feel that old nagging insecurity about my weight creeping back in. I'm tempted to weigh myself but too nervous about the number. I refrain.

But somehow, I suddenly *want* to look perfect for

him. I want him to not be able to resist me or leave me or regret anything.

I slip on a sexy red dress and matching, strappy high heels.

Jackie walks in, wet bathing suit in hand. She tells me about the pool, the servants, the prosciutto and the cantaloupe they served—all that I missed—and oh, followed by only my favorite, wild boar.

"You should have come. You would have loved her… and her house."

"You didn't invite me." I spray perfume on my wrists, look at my hair the mirror and tuck the fly aways behind my ear.

"You were with Fernando! You were late!"

"I was here by eleven!"

"That is late. I wanted to go. You could have called."

"Your phone doesn't work!"

"You could have tried to text. I am getting texts."

I spray my hair with the last remnants of my hair spray, put on lip gloss and leave the bathroom. I'm not going to engage. No drama today with her.

"You know, Fabio was talking to me in the car last night on the way home," she follows me into the bedroom.

"Yes?" I look down as I rub bronzing lotion on my legs.

"He was talking about Fernando. He has had a really rough life. He said his mom died two years ago. And he won't talk about it, really. And his father disappeared and is somewhere in Europe… or is dead. He doesn't know. He is trying to find him. It's so sad, really."

"Yes. I know some of it. He told me about it on the train this morning."

Fiddling with my hair, I exhale the smoke from my cigarette out the bathroom window, hitting one of the pigeons. Good! Die, bird.

"Really? Oh my God."

She brushes her hair and pulls it into a ponytail clip.

"Listen," I light up another cigarette off the first. "I don't want to hear about it. I really don't. I am not his therapist. I was just Henry's therapist. I listened to everything—about his mom's death, the sister he hates. His boss. His colleague who ignores him. I do not care. I do not want to hear anything about him. I don't want to know anything about him."

"You don't?" She looks at me as if I am the evilest of women.

"No, I don't." I take a drag off my cigarette and exhale.

"I don't want to know him. Jackie, I told you, I am here to smoke, drink and fuck. That's it."

"And pour me another Prosecco, please." I grab the bottle out of the bathroom.

"Okay. Okay."

She pours it and turns away. She hates me. She thinks I am a cold-hearted bitch (maybe I am).

I will not be judged. I do not seek her approval. I do not seek the approval of anyone. And I am done giving. Done listening. I am here to *take*. I am here to live my life to the fullest every day. I do not want to know him. I do not want to know anyone.

"Almost there," Fernando texts. "I want to take u 2 Spoleto tonite 4 dinner."

He knows I want to go to Spoleto. It is 30 miles away, and it's where they hold a huge international film festival.

"*Si!*" I text back. "I want to go to Spoleto!"

"Fabio is coming soon too."

"*Bravo!*" I text.

When Fernando arrives, he is in dark-blue, perfectly pressed jeans, an untucked white oxford cloth shirt draped with a navy-and-dark purple striped scarf cascading around his neck. Good Lord. These Italians can fuck *and* dress.

I stand above the patio, at the top of the outside stairs. He walks up to me.

"*Ciao*, darling." He kisses my cheeks, left then right. Then my lips for a bit too long. I can feel the glare of Jackie next to me.

"These are for you. Red roses. Red... red ... just like your dress."

He hands me three red roses. Finally. A man who will bring me flowers. And not for a birthday or anniversary. Just because.

"*Grazie. Grazie mille.* They are beautiful!" I hold them against my chest.

"Bella, you look so beautiful... Ooh la la. What a beautiful dress."

He spins me around.

"*Grazie.*" I smile.

"So, so beautiful," he whispers.

God. Everything is always so beautiful

"I love the scarf!" I twirl it in my fingers. "You look like the Dutch coach!

You know from the World Cup. He had a scarf like that."

He truly is the sweetest man I think I have ever met. He is good—even to my friends. I have watched him pay for everything when we are all together. He even pays for lunch and dinner for Fabio each and every time and tells me it is not a problem. I have seen him talk to children in the street and help elderly women cross over cobblestone roads. I have seen him hold doors open for women and wait patiently as many of them enter a restaurant. I have seen him give his coat to Jackie when she is cold. I honestly don't think he has a mean bone in his body. He seems to just give and give and take nothing in return.

For fuck's sake! I'm starting to feel like Katharine Hepburn in *Summertime.*

Jane Hudson was a secretary from Ohio, lonely independent and curious, who came to Italy to explore what else was out there only to fall in love with a charming Italian man who captured her heart with seductive acts. He turned out to be married and not at all what it appeared to be.

Am I am falling for all of this Italian crap? Am I that much of a stereotype?

Please. Do not compare me to Hepburn. As if she rode her Italian lover doggy style after drinking gallons of wine.

And I am in control and not getting sucked into anything.

I stop myself. Detach. This means nothing. You are not going to get all sentimental now and fall for this guy. This isn't real. It is just a vacation. You don't want to get all attached to him. This is exactly how you got in the situation you did with Henry. You get too attached too quickly and never seem to get out.

Fabio arrives at the house and pulls up music on his iPhone in the living room.

"'Sing me to Sleep!' Morrissey!" Fernando exclaims.

We listen to Morrissey and Bloc Party and Lady Gaga. We drink Sagrantino di Montelfalco, the red wine of Umbria, and light cigars and sit outside on the terrace.

"I do not like this music. I prefer Frank Sinatra," Fabio declares as he exhales cigar smoke.

Fabio is much older than Fernando, but they both share a love for fine red wine and met years ago in Todi at a wine tasting. They became fast friends and seem to be like brothers now.

We laugh because he is requesting what my father would request.

"Okay, play Frank Sinatra!"

I wrap my arms around Fernando's broad neck. He snaps a picture.

Fabio plays "I've Got You Under My Skin."

"Si! Si!" Fernando exclaims.

He pulls me off my chair and toward him, holding my hand as he sits on the patio chair. He looks deep into my eyes and sings loudly. He knows all the words.

I've got you, under my skin. I've got you, deep in the heart of me. So deep in my heart that you're really a part of me. I've got you, under my skin.

He bellows the song in perfect English and kisses my neck.

"Yes, Yes. You are under my skin, my darling."

I laugh. I float. I can't come down.

"Fabio! Fabio," he exclaims, "Put on 'Unforgettable!' Put on that song!"

He starts singing "Unforgettable" out loud to me, pulling my chin close to him. Jackie looks down and quickly flips the pages of a magazine she is reading.

"You are unforgettable." I kiss his cheek.

"No, no, *bella.* You are. So unforgettable." Fernando clenches my hand.

"You will forget me. In a few days, I will be gone, and you will forget all about me."

I squeeze his chin.

"Never. *You are not a woman that is to be forgotten.*"

I'm starting to feel.

Something.

Fuck.

Mariella, the Catholic neighbor, strolls by below us with bags of tomatoes, looking at us with disdain.

"Buona sera!"

I waive to her over the patio. She gives me a dismissive wave accompanied by a scowl.

We decide to take two cars. Fernando has already asked me to spend the night, and Spoleto is closer to his apartment in Terni. Jackie is not happy. She is sick of Fabio. She gives me a dirty look.

"Jackie, relax. Relax." Fernando rubs her shoulders. "It is only 30 kilometers. It is not a problem."

Thirty kilometers is really more like 50 kilometers. We arrive late. It is probably 10:30 at this point. But then, where in the hell do we have to be? I like late dinners. Besides, we don't even get up until eleven here.

When we finally arrive, I start laughing uncontrollably. So does Fernando.

"Jackie is going to *kill* me. Oh my God."

I shut the car door, anticipating the parade of invectives.

We approach the restaurant. It an old stone farmhouse that sits on top a high green hill overlooking farms, and vineyards and tiny houses. It is best place he has taken me to yet.

"Darling," he holds my hand, "this is an agriturisimo. It is a farmhouse and sometimes people sleep here too, but they make all the food here with local ingredients."

"Wow, it's beautiful."

I am thinking it must be incredibly expensive, but he never talks about money, and when I bring it up, he just tells me that it is not a problem. There seems to be endless amounts of everything here—money, wine, food, sex. It's like I can never be satiated.

"Come," he guides me to the edge of the hill, "look at this panoramic view.

I wanted to take you to the place in Italy with the best view."

As I stare out the countryside, I realize how late we are. I look my watch.

"Fernando, we've got to go find Jackie and Fabio. She's going to kill me. We're so late.

"You girls. You have to *relax.* You are in Italy. There is no rush."

He tells me in a very slow cadence. Everything he does, even the way he speaks, is slow and calm and confident.

I rush onto the patio of the restaurant and find their table. Jackie is staring at me with brown eyes full of rage.

"I'm sorry. I'm sorry." I rub her shoulders. "I had no idea it would take this long."

"I'm starving. Had I known we were going to be driving for an hour to eat dinner, I would have eaten a piece of cheese at the house."

"Well, order some bread," I snap. "We'll get some *bruschetta.*"

"I need a glass of wine, now."

She pulls her blue shawl over her shoulders tightly.

"Well, let's order a bottle. What would you like?"

"We haven't ordered anything yet because Fabio has had the wine list and can't seem to make a decision!"

"Fabio! Pick a wine!"

"Seriously, Esme. He has had it for 30 minutes!"

Fernando laughs uncontrollably.

"He just wants to order the right thing for you Jackie. He's taking his time."

"Well, I need a drink Fernando! Just order something, okay?"

"Fernando, stop laughing. Order a bottle." I give him a dirty look.

"Not a problem, " he motions the waitress over, "Yes, we'd like a nice Super Tuscan, please. Do you have the Sassicaia? 2006? Yes, we'll take that."

"Do you always go this far for dinner, Fabio?" She stares him down.

He lights up a cigar.

"Si, si, of course." He leans back in his chair.

"Really? Really?"

"Yes... I drive... 200 kilometers, minimum, for dinner."

"You drive 200 kilometers, for dinner??"

"Yes. Minimum. Sometimes three or four hundred."

Fernando and I split a cod-and-spinach aperitif and then porcini risotto. He splits our food delicately in half, and feeds me the cod with his fork.

Under the table, throughout dinner, Fernando rubs my calf during and places my foot between his legs. I can feel him getting hard, and he laughs at me and rubs my foot. I cannot wait to get back to his place.

"You are so beautiful. You are always beautiful. But tonight, you are *very, very* beautiful. The most beautiful ever."

He tells me this over and over again at dinner. Jackie rolls her eyes and flips through the menu rapidly.

I just take it in. He looks at me with adoring eyes. I feel he is obsessed with me and wants to possess me. I feel gorgeous. I can't get enough of him or all of this attention.

After dinner, I sip the expensive French pink champagne that he has just ordered and eat a slice of cantaloupe. He grabs my leg under the table and rubs my ankle, slides off my shoe, and rubs my foot. I laugh. We know. But no one else knows. Jackie is seated right next to me, but the long white tablecloth hides everything.

"Life is too short for cheap wine, *bella*." He clangs my glass. *"Salute!"*

At the end of the night, we get into his car and drive home listening to more Frank Sinatra. He holds my hand on top of the stick shift. I unzip his pants and pull him into my hand. I kiss his neck up and down as he drives and stroke him up and down. He is erect and moaning. The skin on his uncircumcised cock rolls back, and he presses my hand firmly under his left ball. Despite the skin roll, which I am unaccustomed to, it really is the best cock I have ever felt. It is quite big—perhaps even a bit too big.

"There, there." He presses my hand down further and shifts into third gear as we enter the expressway. There are no speed limits on these country roads, and he drives extremely fast as I kiss his neck and collar bone.

"You drive me crazy." He grabs my chin firmly holding it in place.

It takes forever to park anywhere remotely near his apartment, and it starts to rain very hard. We have to park far away. We dash out of the car, covering our heads with our hands, leaping through puddles on rigid brick roads as the heavy drops dash down. We soar down an alley and up a cobblestone road. I am running out of breath. He is pulling my hand and then my arm. My perfectly straightened hair is sopping wet and matted against my forehead as gusts of wind almost knock me down. My heels are sopping wet and ruined. We're running so fast. I fear I'm going to collapse.

Suddenly, Fernando flings open the glass door, and we rush into the lobby.

We kiss passionately right there and continue in the elevator. He pulls my dress up and then down, dropping rain and making puddles on the marble floor, rubbing my thighs, then rubbing my breasts, kissing my neck. We tear into the apartment and rush into the bedroom. I stop in front of his bed. Slowly and carefully, I take off my heels and align them neatly under his bedroom chair. As I was accustomed to doing at Henry's fastidious home. He kicks them across the room.

I pause.

"Stop. Stop with that!"

He throws me onto the unmade bed. There are still the tangled and soiled sheets of last night. He pulls off my dress, then my panties. His head is on my chest before my bra is even off. I take it off as I try to unbuckle his pants. There is too much time to begin, and there is too little time to end. It will go this way.

There is nothing more than this.

Chapter Seven

Every day is the same, yet every day is unique. He teaches me about Italian architecture. He teaches me to speak Italian. He helps me pick out a purple silk tie for my brother. He takes me to the chapels. Afterwards, he dashes into a little candy store filled with confections and hands me a small dish of Rossella candies—little white sugars cubes filled with cream. (I now keep them on my desk and every so often chew one to remind me of Umbria.) There will be no tailgating. There will be no football games.

Every day I tell myself to savor the moment, but the days are passing so fast. I do not want to go home. It is Thursday. We only have three days left. It is Saturday. There are only two.

I find myself missing him in the few hours we are apart. I think about him all the time. I do not want to miss him. Will not allow myself. Focus. Do not analyze, dissect and wonder. This is SDF. That's all.

* * *

On the final day, we wake up together to the call of the rooster. We are at my house now. Thank God, there are no church bells to remind me of my Catholic mother and my sins.

I wake up with a sense of dread. Much like I do every Monday morning before I have to go to work for the obligatory eight am staff meeting.

"Today is our last day. "Fernando rolls over, drapes his arm around me and whispers in my ear, "I am sad."

"Don't be sad." I smile, turn toward him, and grab his scruffy chin.

"I want you to shave. I do not like this scruff."

"I will shave. You are the captain. I am your commandante. Today is your last day. We will do whatever you want today. Anything you want."

"Good. I like being the captain."

"I am missing you already."

He rubs just below my navel.

"Stop. Do not be sad. We must savor every minute. Let's get up! We don't have much time! Chop. Chop." I grab his arm and sit up.

I am optimism. I am hope. Making the most of it. No time for sadness. I want this day to last forever.

We go out, take a café, and talk about what we will do on this last day. We decide to just hang out in Todi. Stay at the home base, low key. Quite honestly, if you can believe this, I think we are both tired of fucking. In our week together, we fucked in a bed, on a sofa, on a table. We fucked before breakfast. We fucked during breakfast, scattering plates and coffee cups on the floor.

That night, we go to a large open restaurant in the countryside.

We just sit there and stare into each other's eyes. Fernando orders a red, and then another and another.

We share white aged cheeses and spaghetti with a ragu sauce sprinkled lightly basil.

Mostly, I twirl my spaghetti over and over on my fork and stare into his wide saucer brown eyes. Fernando has the widest deepest brown eyes. They are big circles, innocent eyes. But in his gaze, I can see pools of pain, deeply recessed. But sometimes out of the muddy pool, I can see a splash of something full of hope and confidence just waiting to take on the world.

"I don't want you to leave."

He sips his wine slowly twirling it over and over at the bottom. He does everything so *slowly.*

"I don't want to leave," I say.

"I hate it here. It's so boring. The Italians are not interesting. They are not sh-arming like the Americans."

"Charming."

"Sh-arming."

"Charming. Repeat after me! I am the captain!"

We try it again, but he says his throat doesn't work that way. He will never ever be able to say charming.

"America isn't that great. Trust me."

"Yes, it is. You have New York. You have opportunity."

"Yes, we do. And I do believe that you can have whatever you want in America. You can."

"I am leaving Terni. I hate it. I am going to London where my friend Antonio lives. Or I will come to America."

"Anything is possible, darling." I kiss his hand.

And I then, I panic. I believe he is serious about leaving here. I fantasize about living here. But then, really, what could I possibly do here? Open a gelato shop? Make dresses?

"I think I am falling in love with you."

He states calmly over a last sip of wine.

"Do not say that."

"I am."

"You are not."

"Italians… we are… we are *romantic*."

"It is… not possible." I say as I swig back the wine.

"Everything is possible. I am an optimist."

"Well, I am a realist. We barely know each other."

I have said I love you more times than I want to count or care to remember. And not to my parents or my sister. To men who were not worthy of the words.

"I knew it the first night I met you. Everything felt so natural. Didn't you feel it?"

"Stop talking this way. Let's just enjoy our last night." I kiss his cheek.

There will be no love, no sad goodbyes. Fernando has gotten me over Henry. He has shown me a lot of new things. I will be a better person for it when I go home, but I will not fall in love with him.

When we return to Daniel's apartment that night, Jackie is waiting for us. Packing fastidiously. Obsessing over trash that needs taken out and flights that are to occur.

"Is Fernando spending the night?"

She is in her robe, pulling the cord of the trash bag tightly and rinsing out dishes. It is clear I should have been home earlier to help clean up.

"Yes. Of course."

"Did you set your alarm?"

"Yes."

"Does he have an alarm on his cell? Can he set it too?"

"Yes."

"Do think Daniel has an alarm clock in your room?"

She is relentless.

"Jackie, relax. We'll make our fucking flights. And if, for some weird reason we don't, fuck it, we will have another day in Italy."

In some way, I'm hoping the alarm doesn't go off. I will fabricate some excuse for the delay. I have always been good at making things up. Lying to people has always been relatively easy for me.

That night, we have sex and the bed squeals, which I worry about Jackie hearing. It seems passionate, but also desperate. Fernando lies heavily on top of me, almost suffocating me as he kisses my neck over and over again. He becomes violent and throws me on my stomach, holding my arms down tightly and thrusting from behind me. I cannot tell if he is angry or if he is trying hard to make the last time intense and memorable.

My stomach hurts, and I don't know why. I can't focus. I can't sleep. I get up to pee. Again.

"What is wrong, darling?" He rolls over and holds me tightly.

I pull away.

"I don't know. I just don't feel well. My stomach hurts."

"From the dinner, maybe? The garlic?"

"I don't know."

And he lies there and rubs my belly over and over again.

"I do not like goodbyes," he whispers, He is wrapped around me from behind.

"Okay. I understand."

"I do not like long goodbyes. I'm not good at this."

I am now witnessing the beginning of his ability to detach.

"I am not either. We will say goodbye quickly, then."

And suddenly, out of nowhere, I find myself asking him about his parents. Suddenly, in these last hours before I get on a plane to the United States I want to get to *know* him.

"Tell me about your mother. What was she like? What were your parents like?"

"Esme... It is complicated."

"I know... but tell me."

He groans.

"It was not a good thing between my parents. It was not good. I know it is not beautiful thing to say... but it was... it was not good."

"I'm sorry. I'm sorry to ask." I rub his scruffy chin.

"No. No. It is okay. You are... you are just coor-ree-us."

"Curious," I correct him.

"It is cure-ee-us." I enunciate slowly.

"I can't say it! My throat does not move that way," he contends after several futile attempts at trying.

"Si, si, cur-ee-us." I smile at his pronunciation.

I accept it.

He rolls over and lies on top of me. He is a tall broad man, and I feel the pressure of him on my pelvis and stomach.

"It's okay. I want you to *know* me. I want to *know* you."

I just smile. I reveal nothing.

"I will miss you darling," he whispers in my ear

"What will you miss?" I laugh nonchalantly.

"I will miss your beautiful blue eyes. Your beautiful body. The laughs. You have made me very happy these last few days. You have made me laugh a lot."

* * *

My alarm is set for six. Unbeknownst to me, he has set his phone for 5:15.

It is the very early morning. It is dark and still. Even the animals are not awake. His mobile goes off. He jumps up.

"What are you doing? We don't have to get up till six." I roll over.

"I am going to leave... leave now." He stands, quickly pulls on his jeans, and fastens his belt.

"I will get this." I stand, reach for the half-empty bottle of water on the nightstand and the condom on the floor.

"No, no, I have it. I have it," he says.

I let him. I walk him down the winding staircase and to the door.

"*Ciao, ciao*", he says quickly, and rapidly kisses my cheeks. "Tell Jackie *ciao*, okay? And tell her it was very nice meeting her."

"Okay. Okay. I will."

91

"Okay. Okay. *Ciao, bella.*"

He holds my face in his hands for 30 seconds. And then he is gone.

I want to run after him. I want to tell him I will miss him, and these days truly were some of the best in my life. I want to tell him I have to see him again. But I don't. I shut the big brick door between us.

I watch his car stir and the lights go on. I watch it move off following the milky moon.

I finish packing. Gather the sheets. Take out the trash. Wake up Jackie.

And as we drive the two hours to Rome, I do not look back. I will not.

* * *

The Rome airport is jam-packed. I have never seen so many people in one airport in my life. I look at my watch. I start to panic. Fuck! My laissez-faire-ness is finally catching up with me. I'm going to miss my flight! There are lines and people with kids and buses one must take to get to gates. Jackie has to go her gate to the left, and we hug goodbye.

We say all the obligatory things about what a great time it was and how much fun we had, but I know she hates me now and won't likely speak to me again. She never does.

And alas, as I get through all the machinations and security, he is there. On my phone.

"I'm sorry. I left so fast. I am not good at goodbyes."

"It is okay. I understand. I had a great week! *Grazie!*"

I text in a perfunctory and carefree manner.

And I am off to the US of A. To a niece's birthday party. As soon as I land, and a heap of unanswered emails and responsibility. I am filled with dread.

But this is life. I get it.

You have to return to the bad parts to have the good parts. I know this by now.

My sister picks me up.

Chapter Eight

"*Boun giorno*, sister." She hugs me at baggage claim.

"I'm so tired." I sigh. "Let's go find my luggage."

"So, tell me about your trip. Mom said *you met a man.*"

"Well, I did meet the most amazing guy."

I grab suitcase one off the conveyer belt.

"I am sure you did. You're boy crazy."

"What is that supposed to be mean?" I turn about and stare at her.

"Well, I mean, *of course you fell in love.*"

Listen up, hot-pants-New York City-actress-yoga instructor-sealed-the-deal-with-your-gem-of-a-husband-at-29… only to sire unruly, undisciplined offspring three years later—I will not be judged by you.

"Judge not!" I swing my backpack over my shoulder, "Lest ye be judged. And I'm not in love."

Wow. I'm kind of impressed. I'm pulling out lines from Sunday school I never thought I had.

We go to my brother's house for his daughter's fifth birthday party, and I haven't slept in a day. Everyone is full of fucking questions, and the kids want to know what I brought them. Cannot deal now with little children and all these questions.

"How was your trip? How was Italy? Did you go to the Vatican? Did you see the Coliseum? Did you eat lots of Spaghetti Bolognese?"

I find a *vino rosso* and a long yellow slide on the swing set. Catch little nieces as they descend over and over. Tell them how amazing they are.

My brother, Jack, pulls me aside to thank me for the olive oil I brought him.

"This olive oil is amazing, Jack.. This guy Enricho who lived across the street made it himself by hand. Tell me what you guys think!"

"Mom said you met some guy there."

"Yes, yes, I did! He's so amazing, Jack."

"I thought you just broke up with someone four weeks ago. I can't keep these guys straight."

"Fuck you, Jack.." I pour another *vino rosso* and rush back to the slide and the little people. They are my people.

Jack follows me out to the backyard, Bud Light in hand.

"Listen, all you need is a nice normal guy. I have one for you. He's a good guy. On my golf league. An accountant."

"An accountant? Are you kidding me? I hate numbers. And I hate golfers. Forget it!"

"What's wrong with numbers?"

"I don't do numbers. I am writer, Jack.. I do not date accountants."

"Jack, please," my rational sister-in-law, Melanie, approaches us. "Your sister is an intellectual. She is not going date Brian. Get real."

Thank God for Melanie.

My mom and sister-in-law are downing hot dogs and viewing photos in my camera.

95

"Well, you seem to be *very* happy. Wow. I've never seen you hanging on a guy like this. This so isn't you." My Catholic mother asserts her unsolicited opinion as she slaps yet another pile of potato salad on her red shiny paper plate.

"Well, Peg. I was very happy in Italy and having a lot of fun."

"She's always in love. My daughter... my oldest daughter... she is always *in love with love.*" She says this before an audience of relatives and friends. I want to stab her.

So I do.

"No, Mom. I believe in passion. Not love."

I walk away. Fuck her. I know my parents love each other, but I mean, is there really isn't any passion there? She probably never did it on the kitchen floor. She married for practical reasons. And that's fine. But that is *not* how I am going to live my life.

As I enter Jack's kitchen to get some US-of-A macaroni salad (I'm starving) and more wine, my now recently Catholic father approaches me.

"Now that wasn't nice. Your Mom loves you."

"My Mom loves me? Right. She judges me! All you do is judge me. Guess what Lou, I'm done! I'm almost 40 now. I don't care what you think."

"Well, I do agree with your brother. You really need to meet a man here, in our country. And I do agree with your mother. I think you do have a fear of commitment."

"Are you kidding me, Dad? I mean, are you really kidding me?"

I drop the wine and run to the slides. I play hide and seek with the adventurous innocent little people. I show them handmade dresses from Italy and photos from the trip. I can bond with the little people.

"Show me the picture, Esme!!" (I think she too is a little boy-crazy.) Gabriela grabs the camera.

"He's cute. I like him! I told you! You would find another boyfriend!"

They want to go to Italy. They do not judge me. For once, I heart the little children.

* * *

I am now at work. I am jetlagged and hung over from ten days of pure, unadulterated hedonism. My eyes are red and itchy, and there are deep purple rings under them. The Italy glow is gone. I look old again.

I feel irritable and edgy. I don't want to answer questions. I certainly do not want to attend meetings. I just want to go to sleep. There is the boss who is looking for me all the time who likes me to be near him instead of near my computer doing my work. There are the memos. There are emails. There is snail mail. There is a litany of meetings scheduled. I don't know where to begin. I want to slice my wrists.

I keep thinking: *At this time last week, I was doing...*

I check my email. Suddenly:

"So... how was your trip?"

It is an email from fucking Henry.

Fucker. I can't wait to answer it. I can't wait to tell him everything. But I wait.

I think. I construct the perfect response.

Two hours pass.

"*Boun giorno*. Well... in sum, the trip was *amazing*. Actually, when I arrived in Rome, I was sad and missing you very much. The amazing duomos and frescoes didn't do much to assuage the pain. Then, a few days later, I arrived in the countryside, and I met a wonderful man who taught me how to savor sunflowers, sip cappuccinos slowly, and what true passion and romance is all about. I am grateful for the experience. So, allora! I am rested and rejuvenated. And embracing 40 quite well. Be well."

Thirty minutes later.

"I'm glad you had a great trip! It was well needed and well deserved. I'm glad you have finally written me back more than one sentence. I would like us to be friends, if you are down with that. I hope you are doing well. Melatonin helps with the jetlag. Try it."

WTF? But then, what else would I possibly expect to hear from the Robot?

I do not respond. Why would I? He is completely void of emotion.

He is dead to me.

Over the next week, as I finally learn to stay awake and not drink at lunch, I start to reflect. I do not contact Fernando. I try not to think about him at all.

However, I do find that I am nicer at work. I am moving more slowly. I'm less annoyed with the Ph.D-faux-intellectual who always ignores my emails. I'm going out to lunch with my colleagues and actually *talking to them* instead of yelling at them for not making deadlines. I do not feel the same sense of urgency that I used to feel about everything. I think maybe I have changed and perhaps for the better.

Suddenly, one day as I am viewing Facebook and not doing my work yet again, I see the montage of photos that Fernando has posted of our trip. I leap through each one. I go through each and every single one of them over and over again. There are hundreds of them, and at the click of each one, I relive every moment of our time together.

I am still there.

Fernando starts to post on his Wall "amazing week with a wonderful woman!" He tells me to post my photos, and I do. He comments on all of them about how beautiful I am or how amazing I am.

And then it begins.

Constant emails and notes on Facebook, then Gmail. I am no longer working at all. Mining this Facebook operation has become a fulltime job. We quickly move to Skype, and he tells me how much he misses me and must see me again. We are online all the fucking time. By the way, I *know* I am going to get fired. But then, I know I won't. I remind myself that no one here does any work. And trust me, my ten percent is about equal to their 90 percent. I'm sick of giving it my "all" at work anyway. Where has that gotten me?

Somehow, it has escalated to something neither one of us ever expected. I have no idea how this happened, but we start anew across wide oceans and vast lands. We set up Skype dates to talk—on my Saturday mornings before he has to serve lunch at the restaurant, and at midnight his time after he comes home from work and right before I depart for my job.

Then, my dreaded 40th birthday arrives. But today, I am not sad or full of regret. I accept that I'm getting older, and I am simply okay with it. I leave for California at 3:00 for the conference. I'm not going with Henry as I planned, and I really don't care anymore. He hates the sun and would have probably just stressed me out and created some new beach rule.

Fernando and I agree to Skype that day at 1:00 before I depart.

We chat and chat. He wishes me happy birthday. I kind of dismiss it; I just want it to come and go at this point.

"Hold, hold on. I'll be right back." He leaves the screen. I think maybe someone is knocking at his apartment door. He disappears for few minutes, and I can only see the red print above his sofa.

He appears again.

"I made this for your birthday, bella. Happy Birthday! Boun compleanno!"

He has made me a white tiramisu cake, my favorite, and it has three birthday candles on it. He sings happy birthday to me loudly, first in English and then in Italian. I can't stop laughing. It is the best birthday present I have ever gotten in my life. It costs nothing, but it is so genuine and thoughtful.

Happy birthday darling. Now, make a wish, and I will blow out the candle for you."

I make a wish.

"I will blow out the candles for you." And he does. "And I will now eat the cake because I'm hungry."

He laughs and puts into his mouth, white crumbs falling down his lips.

Allora!

It is finally, finally a good birthday.

* * *

As I walk the long white beaches of California, watching the salmon sunset gathering sand dollars, it is quiet. And so finally is my mind. I'm at peace now with 40 and with easing into a new decade. I start to reflect on my life, perhaps half over. And I think about the lessons I learned in Italy.

They are as follows (in no particular order):

1. LAUGH. Laugh a lot, and surround yourself with people who make you laugh. I hadn't laughed as hard as I did in Italy for more years than I can remember. Create a ruckus. Stir it up a bit. Who cares? Life really is difficult, especially when you are a malcontent like me. There is the economy. There are layoffs and re-orgs. Your friends' divorces. Your toxic friends. Your boss who wants to own you. So you really have to find a way to laugh. Laughter is life's elixir. Laughter cures most things. Get rid of the toxic waste sites in your life. Run in the rain. Climb a mountain. Have fun!

Fernando, although far, far away, still sends me emails (albeit in broken English) that make me laugh out such as:

And now... I MISS YOU, I NEED OF YOU!!! very soon we will be together... i had to work so hard because my partener left me...!!! i will buy a new little country house in Arrone, very beautifoul country near Terni and we will sleep there when you will come...VERY ROMANTIC AND GOOD TO MaKE LOVE ALL DAY:::I NEED YOU ON MY BED!!!!!

(I think he means "in" the bed. But maybe not.)

2. NO RULES. There will be Thai. There will be pig. There will be no bedtimes. There will be sex, and there will be breakfast in the morning. There will be days of no plans. It sounds trite—but really do live in

101

the moment. There is no reason for having arbitrary and capricious rules. All these "plans" that cannot be deviated from. Fuck that. Seize the day, and create it as you want it to be, not as you think it needs to be.

3. BE ALERT. There is always someone else out there. Just be watching for him/her. This person really will appear in the place you least expect him or her to be—when you are the least prepared. But pronto! Be alert. They will appear.

4. BE ADORED. There is someone out there who will appreciate your strengths, accept your weaknesses and realize your potential. Someone to adore you. If you do not have this, do not settle. Because one day you will find this. And as my grandfather always told me, it really is better to be alone and happy. One day, when you and the universe are ready for it, he will find you.

5. SAVOR THINGS. In the meantime, savor the things you take for granted. Savor sunflowers, the bite of a ripe, red tomato, a slow smoky kiss. As the Italians taught me, move *slowly*. Savor the simple things. And now, I really do try to drink the coffee at Starbucks in the morning at the bar instead of rushing and getting it "to go." And I am actually "taking" a lunch and leaving my desk for 30 minutes. I'm also trying to look at ferns more.

6. BE OPTIMSITIC. Fernando, who at a young age lost his mother, has the most wonderful outlook on life. He taught me to be an optimist. He taught me to hope. So don't give up on hope. Reinvent yourself. Get the next job. Meet the next guy. You can do it. Put that out into the universe, and believe it or not, the good things you deserve might actually come your way. Fernando taught me that all things are possible.

And come on, it *is* America, and despite Asia rising, all things really are possible here, right?

7. RELAX. I mean, fucking relax. Life isn't about how many hours you bill or how many awards you amass, how many miles you run, how many pounds you lose, how many carbs you don't eat this week—or where you are going to be in the next year. I've spent my life measuring my self-worth according to these metrics. The metrics are wrong. There is a whole wide world out there waiting for you. Sit by the water. Have a glass of wine. Write a poem. Travel. Don't think about the next thing. You can't control it anyway.

8. LET GO! For all those women out there, please do not spend one more nanosecond pissed off at him, obsessing over him... the guy that disappointed you gravely or did you wrong. I get it. I was that girl. Just let go and move on. There is a reason he came into your life, and there is a reason he left. He was a teacher of sorts. Learn from him. And let go.

9. KNOW WHAT YOU WANT. When I met Henry, I didn't know what I wanted. I was all over the map. But honestly, he taught me something. He taught me to recognize what I *don't* want. And that's half the battle. I am grateful for that experience. Lesson learned. And now, finally, I think I am getting closer to knowing what I *do* want.

10. TRY NEW THINGS. Travel everywhere you can. Use that fucking PTO. I let it accumulate and waste over the years. Experience a new country. Eat a pigeon. It will change you for the better. You've got to shake it up a bit, or life can get really predictable and boring.

Recently, I started reiki and am trying to open up my blocked chakras and lay still for an hour. And on

103

Thanksgiving, I have told Fernando I will try something new. I will finally eat his pigeon.

11.DO SOMETHING EVERY DAY THAT SCARES YOU. Fernando took me into an isolated, dense forest for a hike. While I was terrified upon arrival, I got through it, and in the end, it was fucking exhilarating. He has rock climbed, and surfed and touched the sea. He taught me to take risks—big ones, and not calculated ones—and to face your fears. I think I'm going to force myself to learn Power Point now (which terrifies me). I also started flying lessons. There is nothing better than resting in the clouds.

12. PERFECT ON PAPER DOESN'T MEAN PERFECT FOR YOU. I have spent a lifetime trying to get that perfect-on-paper resume. The perfect job, the perfect guy, all the meaningless yet seemingly-important-at-the-time things on my checklist. And I got them. All of them. And I was never ever more miserable. The more prestigious it got and the more I wanted it, the less happy I was. Every single time. In sum, just because it is perfect on paper doesn't mean it is perfect for you. Think outside the box. What is it that you really want? Go for that.

So, that is it.

Or is it?

A text appears from Fernando on my phone while I am on another boring conference call at work:

"I miss you, tanto! I want to talk to you."

I miss him madly, but I am *not* going to say it, and I am not going to write it.

Listen, you can't give your heart up too fast to a guy. They are hunters, and you just let them hunt. Let them chase you till they catch you.

"How are you?" I text back.

"I'm well. Busy. Busy—working a lot. There is so much to do at the restaurant."

"I am so busy too. Work is crazy. I so miss Italy!"

"I want to talk to you… I need to *see* you. We need to Skype."

And we so we continue Skype, again and again. The time difference is challenging. Often, I have to get up early on Sundays. I take my calls in bed. I put on makeup and straighten my hair. I put on a sexy tank top on top of my flannel pajama bottoms. Sometimes, like when on a business trip with luggage lost, I take his calls in a hotel towel.

"Darling… I want to see you. I want to rip off that towel… I want what is underneath."

(QUERY: Is there such a thing as Skype sex? If so, I think we are on the precipice of that.)

Well, for now, we are Sk-ating (Skype + dating). Come on. In so many ways, the virtual world is better than the real one.

And we send each other packages in the mail. I send him movies and CDs from Amazon because we Americans don't have to pay the usurious value-added tax. I send him James Bond crap and the Scorsese collection, an Abercrombie T-shirt, and American bands he has not yet heard of. He sends me lentils (allegedly good for belly flattening, which I so need now) and pesto, Nutella and fresh Parma.

He sends me Youtube songs on Facebook and writes "thinking of you!"

It gets me through the doldrums of work and endless meetings about goals and objectives and spreadsheets on the steps on how to obtain them. I feel like I have spent my entire life writing my goals and objectives instead of living my life and achieving them.

At night, I rush home to get online. It is after midnight his time. I pour a big glass of Chianti. I make a caprese. I slice tomatoes *slowly* and drizzle Enricho, the pork buggy guy's olive oil, over the tomatoes. I am living Italy in my U.S. home as we talk about the events of our day. It is always hard to hang up. We do it *slowly* in Italian style.

"Esme! You are always eating caprese! Always caprese!"

"I know. I know. I cannot cook."

"I will teach you to cook."

"I just got my first nice knife. I cannot even cut a tomato properly!"

"I will teach you darling. It is easy."

"Baci, baci, ciao, ciao, baci, ciao, baci, baci, ciao, ciao!"

(Kisses, kisses, goodbye, goodbye, kisses, goodbye, kisses, kisses, goodbye, goodbye!)

We do this over and over again. The Italians also are not good at goodbyes. It takes at least ten minutes of ciaos every time.

I really miss him. I really miss the sex. I mean I'm going to have to get two pocket rockets now to get me through the interim.

And finally, I have agreed to go there for a week at Thanksgiving to harvest olives. I mean, it is olive season there then. And we are going to harvest them and then make hand-pressed olive oil. (Currently, I am searching for an olive-harvesting outfit.)

My Dad isn't crazy about the idea. I mean, he knows I'm flying to Rome. But he keeps asking me for the "layout" of the boy's apartment and suggesting I get my own hotel. He says I'm being impetuous (again) and that I do not know this boy very well at all. I told him it is way too late for this nonsense. If he wanted to teach me to be a moral and/or normal person, he should have started 20 fucking years ago.

As if.

We are also talking about going to Lisbon for Christmas. We want to eat fish soup on a white beach and drink Port.

Well. Let's see how Thanksgiving goes. For once life in my life, I am not analyzing *any of it.*

But ... I am optimistic.

There are times when I see him on Skype that I think I just may be in love with him. I mean, I know this is what you probably want to hear.

But I am *not* going to be Liz Gilbert here. Remember. This is SDF. So let's just say, we're going to explore it. Okay? I'd like to SDF my way through Portugal next.

In the meantime, I am in America. I continue to just live my life. I run in the mornings, and at night, I write on my blog or have drinks with my girlfriends. On the weekends, I go to farmers' markets and pick out fresh vegetables. I come home to make a proper meal. And now I cut my tomatoes and red peppers *slowly.*

I am just waiting impatiently for November to arrive.

"Only October keeps us apart, darling," Fernando texts me.

Yes, it is October, not April, which as T.S. Eliot attests, that will be the cruelest month.

Last week, after I run a race, I dart off to my best

friend Angelina's daughter's fifth birthday party at her tony country club. Angelina, a former litigator at a top U.S. corporation, has (unlike me) moved on with her life and entered motherhood. She is now a stay-at-home mom of three girls. Per her request, I sent her a draft of this story after I completed it.

As I race in to the club—late, sweaty in running shorts and a sweatshirt—up the dark oak winding staircase, there are 20 little girls in princess dresses sitting placidly in little chairs enjoying a tea party. Their stay-at-home Helicopter Moms hovering over them with digital cameras and balloons in hand.

"Esme! Esme!" Angelina, in her preppy but stylish mom outfit, tracks me down and kisses my cheek.

"Listen, you have to meet my friends! This is Jill, Edie, Jackie, Sara."

My head is swimming.

"Where is the Prosecco?" I whisper. "And where is the food? I'm starving."

"Listen, you guys! This is my friend the writer. The one who wrote the story I sent you... *'Smoke Drink Fuck.'*

"Oh, my God! " They exclaim. "I loved your story!" Sara (I think) says.

"Oh, I want to read this! Can you email it to me?" One random hands me her business card.

"SDF! SDF! SDF!" They all start to chant.

WTF? Good Lord. The stay-at-homes were not exactly my target market. And I *cannot* believe she blast-faxed this to all of *them.*

"SDF baby! I did all three today, can you say the same?" Her wildest mom friend Edie grabs my arm.

Tight black cigarette skirt, ruffled flowered blouse, fishnet hose and black strappy high heels. She is the anti-mother.

Yet, a mother of three boys, she is the hottest MILF I have ever seen. Good Lord. She is hotter than my single friends who have not (and likely will never) conceive one child.

I laugh.

"Hey, you. So, did you like it?"

"I loved it! Are you kidding me?"

"So, I hear you are Skype-ing now? Or you as you say, Sk-ating?

"Yes," I look around anxiously. Where is the fucking pool boy with my cocktail?" I find him with a silver tray.

"Oh, I think that champagne was for me." I swipe it. Down it.

"I know you. You're not Sk-ating... you're Sk-ucking."

"No," I look around (Geez, these stay-at-homes could be Catholics for all I know), "just Sk-ating."

"Whatever," she swigs back her champagne. "You so know you are Sk-ucking."

"Well," I laugh, "not yet. But that *is* probably next."

"Of course, it is! Come on, girl." She grabs my hand. "I'm sick of children. Let's go downstairs and S and D."

And there we go—four ladies, down the stairs to the outside patio. They drill me with questions about the trip, Fernando, the sex, the food, everything. Even I am a bit embarrassed.

"Mr. Winter! Mr. Winter!" Edie motions the club manager over to our patio table.

"Listen, I don't mean to be obnoxious, Mr. Winter, but can you bring us a few smokes?"

"I mean, with all her business here, she really *is* a platinum member," Sara asserts.

"Yes, she really is, Mr. Winter. We don't want proletariat treatment here," I smile at him.

We are getting looks (dirty ones) from the blue hairs at the nearby table.

He hates us. They hate us. I would hate us too.

"We need some smokes," Edie rubs her leg. "Because we are here to launch the book tour—we're here to smoke, drink and fuck!"

"No worries, girls. I'll get you some." Mr. Winter starts to depart.

"And while you're at it… bring some champagne. And some hot strapping young waiters for us to flirt with."

"Listen, Esme, we loved the story. SDF is like Grunge. It's a movement. It's a revolution!" Sara leans in.

"I'm living it each day! *Salute!*" Edie lifts up her champagne glass. We all follow.

My cell buzzes.

"Oh, it's Fernando!" I look at the text. "*Ciao bella, quanto sei bella*!" I read it.

"What did he say?" Edie grabs my phone.

"I don't know. It's Italian?"

"Oh, I lived in Italy for a summer. Let me see."

"Ohhh, how sweet. He said 'how beautiful you are.'"

The girls gush.

"Here, here." She grabs my phone. "Let me text him back."

She begins to type fervently.

"Wait. What are you writing?" I grab the phone.

"Trust me. This is great."

She pulls the phone back on her lap and types, "*Voglio scopare.*"

"*Voglio scopare?*" I read it. "What does that mean?"

She throws her head back laughing.

"He'll know. Trust me!"

"Seriously!" I grab her arm. "What does it mean???"

"I want to fuck you." She sips her champagne.

"What?! Edie!"

Immediately, text received from Italy.

"Very good translation, bella. But a bit boorish."

They crack up.

"He's funny! That is good! It *is* boorish." Sara laughs.

"Oh, my God." I rub my face. "You guys are insane."

The waiter boys show up with silver trays draped with flutes of champagne. "Hello, and thank you," Edie whips a glass off the tray. "Wow, you boys are cute."

"So cute!" Sara chimes in.

They laugh. "Well, we were told you wanted some young men at this table." They stand poised, erect, in little tuxedos, engraved sterling silver trays in hand.

"Indeed we do!" Edie laughs, "I'm a MILF. And she... (she turns to me) she's a Cougar."

"Hyena." I correct her.

"Hyena."

When the club runs out of champagne and we ponder what to order next, Edie jumps up and runs toward the parking lot.

"I know! I know!" She exclaims. "Skinny girl martinis!"

She rushes back with Vodka and a mixer in hand.

"Are you kidding me? You have alcohol in your car?" I look at her incredulously.

"Yes. A minibar in the minivan!"

These stay-at-home moms are uncaged animals.

She fills our champagne flutes with Vodka.

"*Salute*! To Fernando!"

"To Fernando! *Salute*!" They cheer.

"So, when are you going back?" Angelina joins us.

"November. For Thanksgiving."

"Oh, my God. I'm so jealous. I so want an Italian love affair!"

"You have a great life," I admonish her.

"I know. I do. But I want an affair in Italy."

"We want the sequel!" Sara says. "You better write the sequel while you are there."

"Okay. Okay. I will." I smile. I cannot believe this. Edie has already ordered "Smoke Drink Fuck" T-shirts.

Chapter Nine

Fernando keeps asking me what is next for us.

Well. Here's the deal.

He now says he wants to move to the U.S. He had planned his exit out of Italy long before he met me. For a long time, like many potential immigrants, he has sought the American dream—to own his own restaurant here—with 300 customers instead of 30. He wants to get a green card to open up his own restaurant. God knows, we need a decent one in this state.

And I am willing to help him do that. I want the absolute best for him, regardless of what happens with us. I edit his resume and send it back for his review.

I have to delete certain things under "Interests," such as James Bond. James Bond is not an interest.

Recently, he put his restaurant up for sale and has a prospective buyer, a rich soccer player. On his one day off, he goes to the opera and to a museum and then has a cigar and dinner Godfather-style with his best friends.

These Italians. So cultured. There will be no "Pittsburgh Steelers" football games with beer and "the guys" here. They seem to like art as much as being with their girlfriends.

So, right now, a senator's office is now helping me figure this out for him. There are a few options at present. But. Well. It is *complicated.*

The easiest and most expedient route at present appears to be the "Fiancée Visa."

So, you get engaged. And then he can come over here like in six to eight months, assuming the background checks go okay. And they will. I mean, come on! He is no terrorist, and his parents were not in the Weather Underground.

I suspect we can get through the INS. I suspect we can prove love. We have the requisite love emails and photos.

I say, why not? The Fiancée Visa is perfect for me.

Half in, half out. Nothing written in stone. Leave it flexi.

That's sort of how I like things.

For now, I'm just planning my Thanksgiving trip to Italy and trying to help Fernando get all the support he needs to move his life forward in the direction he wants. I talk to potential investors about helping him launch an Italian restaurant. I listen when he complains about how busy he is because his partner has left. I try to leave him alone so he can get all his work done before he closes the restaurant. I check in on him to see how the potential sale of the restaurant is going. I try to satisfy and anticipate his every need.

We can't wait till November. We are in constant communication planning and planning all the fun things we will do when we are together. There is so much to look forward to.

And when I go back to Italy, I plan on writing the second party of our story.

I can't wait to get back to Umbria, a remote piece of land covered with bursting sunflowers, winding brick roads, and rich green olive orchards. This time, Fernando wants to write with me.

"It is 'our' story," Fernando tells me on the phone late at night.

"We will write it together over Thanksgiving. We will rent a house in Arrone, and we will write the second part of your story together, darling."

As the last of the orange autumn leaves drifts to the ground, he texts me:

"Only November stands between us now."

I can't help smiling. It seems I'm smiling all the time these days.

And I am a girl who is perpetually plagued with frowns, squints and smirks.

My friends Daniel and Ellen, the owners of the Todi home I stayed at last August where it all began, plan to fly in from DC. I have convinced them to come to Italy for the holiday. We will all have Thanksgiving dinner together at Fernando's restaurant.

My friend Alessandra is coming from Rome. Antonio and Bridget, his best friends, are flying in from London. Fernando and I are to cook Thanksgiving dinner for seven.

"I will be chef. You will be sous-chef," he says to me.

"I will make a caprese. But I can't really cut tomatoes," I reply.

He knows. A salad. This is about all I can do.

"Always caprese with you! Always caprese. I will teach you. I will teach you how to cut tomatoes. It is easy. *I will show you, darling.*"

115

* * *

Fernando and I plan this trip for three and a half months. We not only plan this trip. We plan *two trips*.

There is not just Thanksgiving. He also makes reservations for Christmas in Portugal, a country that *I* always wanted to visit. He tells me to pick the country—any country—and he would book our flights. Then we will spend New Year's Eve together back in Italy.

During these three and a half months, there are constant notes from Fernando. They come on Facebook. They come via Gmail. They come via text. They come across oceans and time zones and seem to be posted almost every hour of every day. I can't get enough of them.

Some highlights:

I miss you tanto darling! I must see your beautiful face. I need to hear your voice!!! Can we Skype at 6 your time tonight?

I need to see you. I need to hear your beautiful voice! I want you on my bed! 12 more days! I cannot wait to see you.

If you lived in Terni, we would be engaged!

I sent you lenticis today in the mail. I am so sorry I didn't send them earlier, but Italians move so slowly. I couldn't get through the Post today. But I don't want you to ever want for anything. You deserve everything. You are a woman to be loved.

Listen, just trust me. Captain!! Today I am the captain, and you are the commandante. Send me your passport information today! You are moving too slowly. Like an Italian! I need to make our itinerary for Lisbon. Trust me. I will do it all today. Now send it to me! Only November keeps us apart. Soon!!! xxxx

A month before I return, I finally have a draft of the book done. Fernando asks me to email it to him. He asks me for it over and over again. I'm very nervous about sending it to him. He may not like a lot of it. It may not be as *he* remembered it. Maybe this was all in my head. He may think I'm crazy. He may then leave me.

My fear is not unfounded.

I have lost girlfriends over some of the pieces I have written on my blog.

I finally email the story to him late one Sunday night and shut off the computer. It is out there now; the chips will fall where they may. In the morning I wake up early and anxiously check my email.

Fernando1978@gmail.com:

Dear E,

I read over our story and it was great!! i'm feeling better from last night after reading and i don't know really what happened but i think this story that was a joke is the start now is something important for us...i'm happy...to be virtual engaged with you...in our world!!! Your words and your thoughts about us are the same that i would use to describe everything!!! i'm happy to know you and had sex with you. i'm happy that soon I will see you! i'm happy that this isn't just a holiday story! i'm happy you are present and you wants know me! i'm happy—you are real in dc more than any woman in my world! i'm happy to read everything without Antonio's help!!! october will go very fast and we will see the half part of the story, i would read it more and more but now i have the houswife in my appartament to clean and i don't want she sees me crying, because the story drive me crazy!!!!!! bellllaaaaaaa!!!! love! more than you think! Fernando

Such powerful words even though they are merely typed in an online message. *I believe each and every word.* I am happy. I am mesmerized. My words are his words. We are on the same page. The same page on every page...

I am a hopeless romantic. I am a daydreamer. I see the world in a sequence of "what ifs" and "anything is possible" and "you never know." I believe there are no accidents in life. I believe that things happen for a reason ... that people meet for a reason.

I have for sure fallen for him by now, and to me, these words that he writes to me are both meaningful and seductive. They draw me in. I read them over and over again. I cannot stop myself. I never doubt his sincerity. This string of words keeps us bonded tightly together.

I already told you. Fernando was the kindest and most generous man I had ever met. And not just to me—to everyone. I watched him pay over and over again for Fabio and say simply "it is not a problem." I watched him many times pat the heads of little children walking down the cobblestone streets of Terni near his restaurant.

I talk to him on the phone as he chops vegetables and hangs pasta preparing a dinner for his friends. I listen to him cry on phone about his mother's struggle with breast cancer and the long talks he had with her near the end. I read his handwritten cards that come in with big packages filled with pasta and chocolates and a beautiful scarf.

Finally, for once, a good man. I tell everyone about him. I do not have doubts.

Not for one minute.

So here we go. Months of planning. Emails. Skypes. Phone calls. Texts. Every medium of modern technology to keep us together.

Chapter Ten

I am dead tired.

And things are getting very crazy again at work.

Our number two storms into my office and slams the door.

"We are not sustainable. We have to think about sustainability. We are a nonprofit. You have to raise money and soon."

I just want to do my work and be left alone. I have millions of dollars to raise and four grants to write all of which have January deadlines, but there is always this manufactured drama to contend with every single day. And no one will work or even show up for work. The office is often half full. I have never seen anything like this. This would never ever happen in DC. And somehow, I'm supposed to be the one fixing it all. The woman who "reports" to me won't answer my emails and refuses to put pen to paper. I know there will be no one to cover in my absence, and my trip, when I haven't disclosed, is going to piss off everyone.

At night, I just want to go home and pour a big glass of red wine (or four) and watch another episode of *Nurse Jackie*. And then *Entourage*. And then *Californication*. I can't seem to get enough of

Showtime on Demand. I often talk about the characters on the shows as if they are real people when I talk to my girlfriends on the phone late at night. I get attached to Nancy's sister on *Weeds* and feel like I could really give some good advice to Karen on *Californication*. I even get the shows and characters confused because there are so many of them.

Twelve thirty a.m. Fernando's time. The familiar ring on my laptop. The yellow balloon.

"Fernando Adolpho 31" calling.

Fernando has just gotten off of work. I know he is working 24/7 at his restaurant, prepping food early in the morning, managing waitresses and bartenders at night, dealing with customers who come in at random times interrupting our Skypes. I get it. Afterall, I'm busy too and incredibly stressed out from the paranormal shit going down here. Fernando knows I'm going through some major shit at work, but I don't discuss it at length.

"Ciao. Ciao. How are you?"

He appears—smiling widely. His voice soft, breezy, high-pitched. Always carefree and gentle.

He suddenly is right there on my laptop inside my office. Navy blue Abercrombie and Fitch T-shirt with tousled black wavy hair that he keeps smoothing back with his thick fingers. He always worried about his hair and his vaguely receding hairline and the natural part that awkwardly falls smack dab in the middle of his head.

I catch my breath at the sight of him. I think he is the most handsome man I have ever seen. I think he will be that handsome even when every last hair has fallen out of his head.

"Ciao. Ciao. I am fine," I lie. "How are you?"

He sighs and rubs his hair.

"Tired. Just very tired. So busy today at the restaurant."

He leans back against his white leather sofa. A red-and-green oil painting I recognize as his father's work hangs above it.

"Yes. I know. You are working all the time."

"Look at those earrings."

I smile.

"So beautiful. Always so beautiful. I love your white dress. Always in white!"

He leans forward toward me. It feels as if he is right in front of me and I could kiss him.

"I like white."

"I know. When we went hiking that first day, you wore a white dress."

I laugh.

"I didn't know we were going hiking! You failed to tell me that."

He laughs out loud for a long time.

"What are you drinking?"

"Diet Coke."

"Diet Coke. You love Diet Coke. Always drinking soda."

"Because I do not like Coca-Cola Light!"

"You need to shave!" I rub my chin. "I don't like you with all that scruff."

I am always telling him to shave.

"I know. I know. Tomorrow, Captain. Tomorrow I will. You will see. I will call you tomorrow and show you."

He always calls me Captain. He tells me I will call all the shots, and he will do as I wish. Finally. I have met a man who will put my needs first and will do what I want to do.

"I miss you. I never talk to you anymore! You're always working!" I tell him..

"Si, si." He sighs, tugs on his hair.

"I have no partner. You have to understand. I want to talk to you more, but I am always working. Always working. I am not on the PC all the time like you. I am in the kitchen cooking. Always customers."

He seems irritated.

He rubs his hair and sighs. I know that the sudden departure of his partner, Romeo, has left him overwhelmed and exhausted. I try not to push it. The demands of the restaurant in many ways is starting to pull us apart.

"I know. I know."

"And the PC... it never works here. Our wireless! The Italians... Ugh. I am not good with the computer. I will have Allejandro help me tomorrow."

"Okay. Okay. See if he can help."

Normally, I would give up on this. I mean under *any* other set of circumstances, I would. The communication. The language barrier. The time difference. It is always going to suck.

"How are things with you? Did you get your blood tests back? What did the doctor say? Tell me. I have been worried about you."

I have been so tired. More tired than I can remember in ages. I was convinced I had a Vitamin D deficiency or anemia. I went through a series of blood tests. The results came back perfect. He has been emailing me about this nonstop. He tells me that he is very worried about me and wants me to call him after the doctor.

"It's fine. Fine. It was nothing."

"Nothing? Are you sure?"

"Yes. Yes. Turns out... I'm just tired." I smile.

"Things still bad at work?"

"Si, si." I sigh. I shake my head.

"Do not worry. It is not worth discussing."

"What is it? What is wrong?"

"I don't want to talk about it."

"Tell me. I want to know."

"He's just crazy here right now, Fernando."

"Like what?"

"I just work with a bunch of lazy people. They won't do any work. And I keep getting told I have to fix it—to raise money. There's an enormous amount of pressure to raise money."

I don't want to talk about it. He isn't going to understand fundraising and dealing with Members of Congress and writing federal grants. And I don't have the energy nor interest in explaining it. Work, which used to be the most important thing in my life, is barely holding my interest anymore.

"It isn't worth talking about. Just forget it."

"Jesus. You need to quit. You are too smart for this. You need to be your own boss!"

"I know. I know. I think I want to be a way-treese in your restaurant." I laugh.

It actually sounds far easier and much more rewarding at this point. I could cut tomatoes and make pasta. I kind of know how to now, and I was a good waitress in college. I have a really good memory.

"No! No dearling! There is no money in restaurants... I love what I do... but there is no money."

"Here... 30 customers. In New York or DC... 300 customers."

"Well, at least you are the boss."

"Yes. I am the boss." He laughs. "I am a mean boss, too."

"No, you're not. You are not mean, Fernando."

I am a girl who can be mean. I am a girl who knows anger. I know how to cuss, and I know how to go for the jugular. But I can honestly say I have never seen one act of meanness from this man. I don't even think he is a person who can be mean. Like he's too mellow for anger and all that overreacting…

He laughs.

"Listen to me. You need to send me your passport information so we can go away at Christmas. I want to book our trip. I'm serious."

An internal voice, the one I often choose to ignore says, *Red flag. It's too soon. Don't you dare book another ticket. Just see how Thanksgiving goes. Move slowly.*

"Where do you want to go? Barcelona still?"

"I don't know."

"Well… where? Where have you always wanted to go?"

"Portugal." I smile.

"Liz-bon! Si, si. Si!!! Let's go to Liz-bon. You have never been?"

"No."

"It is beau-tee-ful. So beau-tee-ful. White beaches. Port. We will drink Port on the ocean. Por-tu-gay-zee… such a beautiful language."

"Well. Let's talk about it later. Let's just see. Thanksgiving is soon."

"Only a month now. Only October keeps us apart."

"Yes. October is the cruelest month." I smile.

Actually, I have always contended that it is February is the worst month. February is cold and dark and full of black. And you never ever know when Spring will arrive.

February also contains Valentine's Day. And I always seem to break up with someone right before February 14th. I hate February. But right now I'm hating November more. It really is the cruelest longest month. And there are 30 days in it, not 28.

"I know. I know. I cannot wait."

And it really is all I am living for now. I can't wait to escape this drama at work.

"I am working a lot now because I am going to rent us a house in Arrone."

"Why? We can stay in Terni in your apartment."

"No, no. We will go to Arrone. To a romantic villa. It is small. There will be only a bed and a bathroom. But it is beautiful there. Panoramic view. We will be alone. Have champagne... romantic dinners... make love."

I have no fucking idea where this Arrone is, but it sounds amazing.

"Where is Arrone?"

"Not far from here. About ten miles outside Terni. In the country. It is beautiful. We will be away from everything and everyone. I want to be alone with you."

I hit Google Maps as we talk, but Arrone doesn't even come up. However, Wikipedia reports that the town was founded by Arrone, a nobleman from Rome, in the 9th century first as a wooden castle, which was later built in stone. The Arroni family was later ousted by some dude from Spoleto a few centuries later. Then, the town was sacked and set on fire by the French troops in 1799.

Sounds pretty fucking glamorous. A castle. An ousting. A fire. The French. I think it sounds like the perfect place.

"Well, okay, but Antonio is flying in from London. He and Bridget have a lot of plans for us and…"

"We'll see Antonio. But I want us to be alone too."

He is firm and seems annoyed with Antonio's proposed itineraries and plans.

"Okay. Okay."

"I have been so busy. I bought a new bed today." He laughs. "It is not a big bed though. It is… for about one and a half. We will have to sleep *vicini, vincini.*" (Near, near.)

"Okay. It's okay." I laugh.

My boss knocks on my door.

"I have to go! I have to work now. Ciao. Ciao."

"Ciao. Ciao. Baci baci, ciao, ciao." He kisses the screen.

"Baci, Baci, Ciao." I blow a kiss.

"Baci, Baci, Ciao, Ciao, Baci." He blows another kiss.

Italians can never ever say goodbye.

I quickly slam the lid of my computer. I now have to go back to drama at work reserved for Directors and VPs. How in the hell did I get involved in this anyway? And when did I suddenly become part of the senior leadership team? I so want to go back to middle management.

God. I just want to write my love story and be left alone.

Preferably in Italy. With Fernando.

* * *

The next day Fernando sends me three emails. He is pressing me very hard about this Portugal trip. Antonio helps us organize it. There are too many logistics and language barriers between us. Although an Italian from the same village, Antonio did his residency in London and is now a psychiatrist there. He tells me often that I have brought out the best in Fernando and given him a zest for life that he previously lacked. He wishes us a long happy life together in America. He is always so positive, so certain about things between the two of us. And he is his best friend. He would know, right?

I tell Antonio to forget it—the flight to Portugal is way too long, I'd have to change planes in Amsterdam. It's too expensive. Antonio suggests and Fernando agrees that I should fly direct to Rome on December 23rd and we will then go to Portugal for four days and return to Italy for New Year's. He can only take a few days off from work. I still do not agree. I mean, this is another thousand dollars, but he can't close down the restaurant again for a week. And I do have all this PTO. And who wouldn't want to spend the holidays in Europe? I see my family all the time now anyway, and they are getting on my fucking nerves especially with all this judgment about my international romance.

My mother constantly calls me telling me that I

am crazy and that I should not be booking two flights. My sister texts me daily that I should make him chase me and not purchase another flight to Europe. My father reiterates that I should get a hotel and have my own place in Terni.

Fernando Email Number 1. Sent 3:34 a.m.

Lisbon! Send me your information! Rapido!

Email Number 2. Sent 1:30 p.m.

I am just waking up...

Dearling! Listen to me! Just send me your passport information. I will take care of everything. Trust me. Just let me do it. And send it soon!!!!! You are like an Italian. You move slowly!!!!! Send it today! I need to book our itinerary!" Ciao, baci, baci. xxx

I do not respond. I am nervous about this second trip before we've even had the first one.

Email Number 3. Sent 6:30 p.m.

I am at a boring business lunch with banal self-absorbed people who tout their degrees and titles. They are going on and on about something in today's *Wall Street Journal* about United Healthcare and a possible merger. I can't focus on the conversation. My duck confit salad has lost its appeal. I go to the restroom and check my email.

Where are you? I want to go to Lisbon with you

for Christmas! Send me your information! I need to book the hotel. Trust me!!! I will take care of everything. Send today!!!

God. Lisbon sounds a whole lot better than this boring lunch and boring life. I swear. I think half of the situations I get myself into are due to pure fucking boredom. This virtual life I have managed to create for myself is anything but boring.

Finally, I cave. I call my mom's best friend, Linda, who is my travel agent. She is against this whole thing, to put it mildly. She is a world traveler. She has been everywhere. She says in a foreign country, trust no one! And she feels strongly that things between Fernando and me are moving too fast. She already booked the Thanksgiving ticket for me, and she tells me to think about the second one.

"You don't even know this boy. Make him come here. And if you are going over there for Thanksgiving, then you need to get your own hotel."

I laugh and tell her not to be jealous of my life.

My dad constantly brings up the hotel thing as we are looking at Audis as I am in desperate need of a new car. I'm trying to concentrate on things like gas mileage and warranties, and he won't stop talking about the trip.

"Leave me alone, Dad! I'm going to stay with him. I'm going to be with him all the time anyway. It's stupid to get a hotel."

"Just get a hotel. It will make me feel better, and you don't even know him that well. What if something goes wrong?"

"Nothing will go wrong!"

After not finding nor agreeing on a car, we stop on the way home to pick up sushi. As we sit down to eat, my mother decides to insert her opinion.

"Well, I agree with Linda," my mom chimes in as she shoves overpriced, mediocre sushi down her throat.

"You don't really know him all that well."

"Whatever, Mom. We are going to have a romantic beautiful holiday in Arrone."

"Whatever." She rolls her eyes and swigs back her Malbec.

My dad gets up and goes into the kitchen to pour another Vodka.

"You are just jealous. You have never know true passion and love." I whisper "I don't need true passion and love at my age! I mean, what the hell Esme? I am 65 years old. Do you really think I want to roll around on the kitchen floor and have sex at this point in my life? I just want to golf with my girlfriends."

"See? You married for pragmatic reasons! You wanted to have kids. Be a doctor's wife!"

"You are too romantic. You are such a dreamer."

"I'm a writer, Mom. We dream. We have to dream, and then we write about our dreams."

"Well, you need to be more realistic. I really do not think you should be going to Portugal. I agree with Linda. Make him come here."

"Why? I already live in America. I prefer Europe. Plus, he can't close the restaurant that long, and I have the vacation time."

Query: Why does everyone always say that? "Make him come here?" Why would I do that? What is so great about America? Childhood obesity everywhere?

131

Moms who were flannel pajamas bottoms to the grocery store? Cheeseburgers? The Super Bowl? And then you're supposed to send your sons and daughters off to not one but two manufactured wars only to lose their limbs without a G.I. Bill and return to this great America? Please. Forget it. He's not coming here. I don't even want to be here.

"You are in love with love! Not with him." She tucks her bobbed red hair behind her eyes and purses her lips.

"You're in love with money!" I say.

She swigs her wine, slices her tuna tartar in half and dips it slowly in soy sauce. . Linda and my Mom worry. They know more about men than I do. They converse regularly. They have even learned to text, and they send each other messages about how crazy I am. Finally, I tell Linda to book the flight. I give her my credit card, already burdened with the other unpaid ticket. And a lot of clothes that I'll need for the trips.

I give Fernando my passport information. All of it.

Without reservation.

He is delighted. He texts:

"Your middle name... it is Maria. Maria," he texts.

"Yes. So what?"

"I love it. I love Maria. You will always be Maria to me," he texts back.

"I'm so happy. I booked our flights for December 24th, and a hotel. Check your mail."

"I'm happy too :)"

"I want to know you, Maria. I want to know everything about you."

And there it is. A link to an amazing five-star hotel in Portugal. I click and click and click scour through all the pages. It has this very eclectic bar with statues of Ganesh. It is India and Portugal mixed. I will have chicken tikka and a big glass of Port at the five-star.

I can't wait. I just want to be there and with Fernando. I wish we could just skip Thanksgiving and get right to Christmas. I just want to go to Lisbon. I want to eat fish soup and drink Port. And for once in a very, very long time, I am excited for the holidays. I will spend all three of them overseas with Fernando. My friends are jealous. My dermatologist, and her assistants are jealous.

"I can't believe you are going to Italy again." Dr. Norman says as she inserts a vile of Botox into my forehead.

"I know. I'm so lucky. Isn't it awesome?"

"Totally, now scrunch your eyebrows. Make a furrowed brow."

"You have to send pictures! I want to her all about it, her assistant grabs my hand.

"I mean my husband does nothing. Nothing. I do everything around the house, for the kids. I don't even want to sleep with him anymore."

"My husband does nothing either," Dr. Norman fills up the needle "I pay all the bills. Walk the dog. Teach classes at night. It's so exhausting."

"Run to Italy! Just go!"

For once, everyone wants my life.

I thank God every day. I am so grateful. I feel that I am the luckiest girl in the world.

I do not take one minute of it for granted.

The days approach. It is the third week of October. It is the fourth. We Skype. We text. We email. We plan. We count the days.

We make so many plans. There will be days

alone in Arrone. Days of shopping for cashmere in Orvietto. Days of harvesting olives and drinking red wine in Montefalco. We will drink a certain type of champagne that Antonio will bring from London. A daytrip alone to Spoleto where an international film festival is held each year.

I can't even keep up with all the plans.

Suddenly, we are in November. Only three weeks to go.

And as we enter this month, there is a subtle but palpable change in the state of things.

My talks with Fernando become less frequent. He doesn't text me or email me that often. He always seems so busy with the restaurant. I don't want to bug him. I don't want to be needy. I know he is working all the time so he can close the restaurant for the week that I am there. He frequently reminds me of this.

I try to put it aside. I can't really deal with much now anyway. I'm working a lot. Dealing with the work and our sustainability issues. Traveling for work. Writing grants on the weekends. It seems I am at the computer all the time, just working and writing.

I just figure I'll bury my head and work hard until November 23rd, and that is what I do.

But I am a girl. And even when we try to detach and not worry, we worry. We analyze. We think about it—a lot. We dissect every single thing with our girlfriends. And I start to do this. I know I'm probably putting negative vibes into the universe. I tell myself I'm sabotaging things again. I tell myself to just relax. My friends tell me I'm creating drama and that he is just very busy. Be patient. You just need to see each other. You just need to talk face to face.

I go to lunch with Gianna and Jill, my best friends from college. We are hung over from last night which consisted of myriad bottles of red wine and hummus at the local wine bar. We order chicken enchiladas and pints of draft Microbrewed beers.

Gianna is now finally happily married but desperately wants a child, and it just isn't happening. Jill has three beautiful children and a crap husband and a nasty divorce in the works. I am single, probably on the verge of losing my job for failure to meet expectations and dealing with a crazy romance in Italy with a guy who appears to be detaching from me.

"You should not go to Italy. Cancel this trip. Spend Thanksgiving with me." "You don't understand. He is so sweet. Truly. Like, he sent me this amazing package of food from Italy—pasta, pesto and lentils. And we Skype all the time, and he tells me how much he misses me and can't wait for November. And he booked these flights and how we would be engaged if I lived in Terni and…"

Gianna interrupts me.

"Do what you want. Fuck him if you want to. Marry him. I don't care. I'm here to support you."

Gianna is an Italian. She knows her people.

"I mean, I don't care. I really don't. My aunt met her husband in south of France. She was from Italy, and he was German. They made it work. Stranger things have happened."

She chugs her beer and dips a tortilla chip in guacamole. I start to down chip and after chip. I even skip the salsa.

"And Jill, I wrote this novel about our first trip together. And he read it. You didn't read it but…"

135

"I can't read it. Seriously, I have three kids. I'm always grading papers. I can barely keep my head above water."

She rolls her eyes. I love these women with kids. They are always *sooo* busy. Like who isn't? Learn how to multitask. And read a book!

"Whatever. Okay, fine. But he read it, and he said it was beautiful. And that it made him cry."

She takes a big gulp of her beer and laughs.

"Of course he cried! He was like, "I got myself a live one here. A crazy one. I'm getting my green card! I'm coming to America now! I hit the gold mine!'"

I literally spit water the water in my mouth on the table and choke on ice. It is quite possibly true. The thought hasn't not entered my mind more than once.

"Seriously, dude. If you fall in love over there and decide to bring this immigrant over, you better sign a prenup and protect your assets," Jill continues.

"We're not getting married. Stop. We'll just see how November goes, okay?"

"Okay, crazy girl. I know you. He's going to rope you into something…"

"So, let her green card him, Jill. Who cares? PJ can help him set up an Italian restaurant here. God knows we need one. And then she can divorce him if she wants."

"At least I'll have two years of unbridled passion."

I smile. Gianna and I toast.

I come home. My mind is racing as it often does. I cannot quiet my mind.

I pour a red. I call my friend Anna in New York City. She is a high-powered Wall Street (what remains of it) lawyer, rail thin, driven as hell, tough as nails, and the eternal pessimist. She is *always* skeptical; she trusts no one.

She is the worst person I could call now.

But I call her because I'm kind of losing my mind, and I really can't think of anyone else to call. I need someone to talk me down off the ledge.

"How do you know he booked these tickets to Portugal? Did he ever send the itinerary?"

She inhales her cigarette on her new Upper East Side apartment balcony. I can just *see* her sitting there all Kissinger-esque—paranoid and skeptical, predicting the absolute worst.

"No! Stop it, Anna. Why are you even talking about Portugal? You're making things worse. I'm fucking on Italy right now, okay? And Thanksgiving. I just want to know what you think about the fact that he isn't emailing me as much. I mean do you think I should go to Italy?"

"Well, it's not good."

"This from a girl who went to Vietnam, Cambodia and Laos with a British guy she met in China on vacation only three weeks before. Please. As if you should be judging me right now."

"That's exactly why I should be judging you. I went to Vietnam with some guy I barely knew, and he turned out to be a boring Midwestern Dad who didn't even want to drink. I left him as soon as I got to Cambodia. We lasted four days! You need to make sure it is okay *before* you get to Italy."

"Whatever. You're paranoid. I do *not* want to be like you Anna!"

"I'm not *judging* you. I'm just telling you that

you need to figure it out. It wasn't a good situation for me. In fact, I had to leave him after he got all those clothes made for me."

"I can't believe you left him in Vietnam."

"Cambodia." She laughs.

"Well, what do you want me to do?"

"Pick up the phone and call him. You guys are grownups. No more emails."

"I did call him yesterday. He didn't answer. He didn't call me back."

"Call him again. You need to figure this out before you get on a plane to Italy."

"Anna, I agree with you. But how am I supposed to talk to him if he won't call me back?"

"Keep trying. He'll call you back. Come on."

She abruptly changes the subject.

"Listen, I have to tell you about this Economics professor I met. He's a total libertarian just like me… I'm reading his book right now, and he's…"

I tune out. I cannot deal with the professor at this moment. I cannot deal with little Miss Anna/Ayn Rand. I have to figure out very soon if I am going to get on that fucking plane.

During the day, Antonio and I email all the time. He is our interpreter. He is my friend now too. He is a kind man. He tells me Fernando is so happy since he met me and how he hopes for the best for us. He reassures me that everything is fine. I believe him. I mean, he is his best friend and a fucking shrink to boot. He tells me over and over again that Fernando is excited about my arrival and planning to close the restaurant for a week, which he never ever does. Antonio is so proud of Italy and tells me about all the wonderful things the four of us will do, so not to worry.

So I don't. There is a big festival in Terni November 7th through 14th. Fernando warns me he won't be able to talk a lot during this time. Nonetheless, he does send me emails. Just less romantic ones—there is no more baci baci. There is just ciao.

I notice it.

November 10th.

It is Friday after work. I can't analyze it anymore. I can't keep surmising and conjecturing. I pick up the phone and call him. I do the improbable for me—a consummate conflict avoider. I bring it up.

"Ciao, ciao," he answers.

"Are you busy? Is this a good time?"

I pull my car over in front of the farmer's market that I go to after work to get fresh vegetables and fish. I cook all the time now. Fernando has taught me, a girl perpetually plagued with eating disorders and rituals on how to avoid calories, how to cook and just eat and enjoy it.

"Si, si. How are you?'

"I'm good. How are you?"

He starts to talk, goes on and on about the restaurant, how busy he is... how tired he is. How he may have a buyer for the restaurant. How a soccer player is interested in buying it. How he and the coach came by today.

"Listen," I stop him. "Listen to me."

He stops.

"We need to talk. Listen, I'm coming soon, and

we... just don't talk anymore. And I just feel this distance between us. Like a real distance. And if this isn't what you want... if you don't want me to come... just tell me, okay? Just tell me. It's okay. Maybe I shouldn't come. I'm thinking maybe I shouldn't come?"

Silence.

"I mean.... there is this distance between us, no? You don't even seem excited anymore. I mean, do you even want me to come?"

"Of course. Of course."

He goes into his higher pitched, breathy voice. He seems shocked.

"Darling, of course I want you to come. I rented a house for us in Arrone—for just the two of us. I've got the tickets to Portugal. I planned my holidays around you. I've planned *my life* around you. How can you think this? I've planned everything around you."

He raises his voice. He again seems irritated with me. I fear I have again overreacted and am being insecure.

" It just seems very different between us."

"No. No. I'm just working... working all the time. You don't understand. Be patient. Soon you will be here, and it will be good. I'm working so I can close the restaurant for seven days. For you. For us. So we can have this holiday together. I need holiday."

I say nothing. I am trying to believe him.

"You have to be patient, Esme. *Be patient.*"

I can't think of anything to say. People have been telling me to be patient since I was five years old.

"You're angry with me?" he teases and laughs.

"Si, si. I am angry."

He laughs.

"Don't be angry with me. Please. I want you to love me. Don't be mad at me. Just love me."

I say nothing.

"Listen. Listen to me. Remember the first night I met you?

"Si, si."

"I told you I wanted to move to London. I told you I was going to leave Italy and move to London."

"Yes. I remember."

"But then... then I met you. And then this beautiful door opened. This beautiful door to you... to America. Now I want to be with you. You changed everything. Can't you see that?"

I'm not sure about America. I know we have been talking about the Fiancee VISA, but now I'm not sure. I don't think we should be making decisions of that magnitude until we see each other in November.

A few weeks ago, he told me he wanted to move here. He asked me to call an immigration lawyer. I talked to a senator that I used to work for and then my friend at the State Department. I got all the information. I know how to get things done. I believe that anything is possible and where there is a will, there is a way.

I gave Fernando the options over Skype.

He said he and Antonio were going to go to Rome to fill out the immigration papers for the "investor visa" that I recently found out about. I told him to stop. Don't go to Rome. Not yet.

"Why? Antonio will help me with the English. He will help me fill out the paperwork."

"Fernando, listen to me. Listen. You can't fuck

this up. You have only one chance with the State Department. You have to wait. You have to wait till you sell the restaurant, till you have money and real investors. We'll talk about it in November."

He agreed to wait. I force him to wait. Things are getting out of control, and I don't really know how to stop it. I keep telling him that we need to talk about things more when we see each other in November.

"I want you to come. In November, we will be together. It will be good then. We will have romantic dinners, and we will cook Thanksgiving dinner for Daniel and Ellen and Antonio and Bridget. We will make love all day, and have champagne at night."

He is always full of smiles. He is so convincing. So fucking convincing.

"Okay, okay," I concede.

"I'm sorry. I have just been a bit dee-pressed lately."

"Why? Why are you depressed?"

Depressed? Isn't that my role? He is always all smiles and relax and food and wine and naps.

"It's the restaurant," he sighs. "Romeo is gone. I have no partner now. It's so busy. I want to get out of Italy. I hate it. It's so boring. The people are so stupid. They move slowly, and they are not sh-arming like you and Daniel and Ellen."

"Listen to me. You can change your life. Anyone can if they want to. I believe where there is a will there is a way."

There I go again.

"Si, si." He laughs. "You are an optimist… always an optimist. You are right. Where there is a will there is a way. You always make me feel better."

I lift him up. I give him hope. I become his cheerleader. He is slowly becoming an emotional vampire. He is starting to take it all out of me just like Henry did.

Fernando has always been laid back and calm. I am high-strung and running a million miles an hour. I am easy to agitate and can lose it at a moment's notice.

Yet…we both love Paul Auster, and the violin, and food and wine and traveling and American literature, and I can't keep my hands off of him. It feels like destiny. I think he is the most interesting man I have ever met. He certainly isn't like anyone else.

So I agree to go to Italy. I agree not to be angry anymore. Fernando tells me absolutely everything I want to hear. He calms me down.

* * *

Several days later, he has a sudden 9.0-on-the-Richter-scale fight with Fabio. I can't understand this, as they were always so close, like brothers really. When I was in Italy, they spent every day together. Always on the phone and always texting. Daniel, who has subsequently spent a lot time with both of them, said he thought they were like brothers as well. Daniel keeps asking me how this could be.

I hate fucking Facebook, by the way. I need to drop off this thing. Fabio has just joined. This is truly the source of a lot of my problems right now.

Antonio contends Fabio and Fernando are on Facebook for the first time now because the Americans who visited him have given them a new zest for life, and Fabio really wants to keep in touch with people now. Fernando has given him a laptop

Then suddenly there is some blow out. And Fabio starts to constantly write mean things about Fernando on my wall. He knows he will see it.

"ESME… you must get rid of restaurant owners. They are the worse!!!"

"Do not ever talk to a man from Terni, Italy!"

He keeps writing these weird things over and over.

This *is* so immature by the way. I know this. But when you are millions of miles apart, these Internet sites are what keep you all linked together.

Fernando Skypes me immediately. He is angry. He keeps rubbing his hands through his tousled black hair and rubbing his cheeks.

"Why are you talking to him? Why is he writing on your wall? Why is he writing these things?"

He is enraged. I have never seen him like this.

"Listen, I don't know. Stop yelling at me! I can't control what he writes on my wall. I don't even know what is going on."

"You need to defriend him. You need to be loyal to me."

"Fine. Fine. I don't care, okay? Just stop this. It's nonsense."

"I don't want you to be friends with him."

"I don't even know how to defriend him."

And I really don't. I'm really not that Facebook-savvy although I should be by now. I can barely crop a picture.

"You need to get rid of him. All of my other friends did. If you want to see him in Italy when you come, you can. I won't see him. You can go off with him on your own."

"I'm not going to see him! I don't care about him. I'm coming to see *you*. What in the hell happened?"

"He came in to the restaurant with Antonio and Mateo and Allejandro. To have lunch. They were here all afternoon. Drinking and eating and smoking cigars… and they left rubbish everywhere. And they did not tip the wait-treese. And I sent them an email… they are no longer welcome as friends here. Only customers. That is it. They have no manners. No manners at all. They are disrespectful!"

"Well, okay, but I'm sure Fabio feels bad. I will tell him to say he's sorry and bring a tip for her. That is the right thing to do."

"NO! You cannot talk to him about this! Do you understand? I'm telling you this in confidence. Do *not* talk to him! My friends warned me not to tell you! They think you are talking to him!"

"I don't fucking care what your friends say about me."

"Do not write to him."

"Fernando… seriously. You guys are acting like 13-year old girls. This is ridiculous. I don't want to talk about this anymore."

"I am done with him! Fabio is the devil! You need to defriend him. You are with me, not him."

I hang up. This is crazy. But, in my mind, I kind of attribute it to Italian drama. I mean come on, what American guy would even engage in this type of dialogue? Would my meathead golfer brother? Fuck no. He just wouldn't hang out with the guy anymore. They would never write one thing on any guy's wall. But there are cultural differences. And these guys are like the characters in *The Godfather*. Obsessed with loyalty

145

and honor. So I figure this is what this is about. That is how I rationalize it to myself, but still, I feel something isn't quite right. This reaction of his is so severe.

I should have paid attention.

Fernando cuts Fabio completely out of his life. He tells me he will never see him again because he is not respectful. That is it. He sees the world in good and evil. Black and white. And suddenly, Fabio is now evil.

It is done.

I cannot bring Fabio up, or Fernando goes into a rage. I do not bring it up.

In retrospect, I know I should have seen this as a big red flag. He cut a person he loved out of his life for a minor transgression. But I don't see it this way. I see it the way I want to see it.

We are now a week away from the trip. In seven days, I can escape and return to the man and country I love. Escape work and the drama that has ensued. Escape my family. I am dead tired. I just want to have some fun.

I hear nothing from Fernando the week before I am supposed to leave. Not Monday. Not Tuesday. I already told you I felt something was wrong. But Antonio and my friends keep telling me over and over again that he is just working so hard in the restaurant so he can close it when I come and I am overreacting. I don't think they're right, but I try to believe them.

"Just call him. You can work this out," my best gay guy friend George tells me. "I mean, this email and Facebook stuff is ridiculous. We are not 23 years old. We are adults. Just call him."

I cannot sleep. So finally one night I wake up at

4:00 a.m., figuring it is 10:00 a.m. his time. It is a good time to call. So I do. He does not answer. There is no voice mail. He used to always text me back right away after I called if he couldn't answer.

"I want to talk to you, but a customer is here. I'll call you in an hour."

But he doesn't text. He doesn't call me back.

It's now Thursday. I am leaving in four days. I text him. I email him:

"We need to talk about my itinerary, about where we will meet in Rome. Where are you?"

He has my itinerary. He has always had it. He always tells me the same thing.

"I know dearling. You arrive on the 23rd of November. At 9:00. I will get you and we will go to Arrone."

He never calls. By Friday, I am totally losing it. I call Antonio.

I pace on my wet patio smoking cigarette after cigarette.

"Antonio, I know something is wrong. He isn't answering his phone. I don't think I should come to Italy."

I step on my cigarette and immediately light up another one.

"Do not worry. It is okay. He is working very hard now. I just spoke to him last week. It will be fine once you get to Italy.

"I don't know if I should come. What if he doesn't want to see me?"

"Just come to Italy. Trust me. It will all be fine when you get here. We will have a wonderful time. He has made so many plans."

I start to panic. I check my email and phone constantly. I pace. I begin smoking again on the patio. You know how this is when a guy does this to you and makes you go fucking crazy.

So Antonio calls. He has spoken to him but only briefly.

Fernando has said only this: "I am overwhelmed. I cannot cope. I need to get away."

Antonio reports back.

"Is he not picking me up in Rome? Is he not coming to get me? Why? How could he do this?

"I'm very sorry. Very sorry."

"I'm not going to go to Italy. Tell me why he did this, Antonio. I know you know. Just tell me." I'm trying not to lose my mind, but I know I am going mad. Did he meet someone? Just tell me."

"I don't know. I don't understand it. He didn't tell me much. But yes, you have to come. Bridget and I have plans for you and Fernando. We will go without him."

"He has to have met someone, Antonio. Just tell me. Did he?"

"No. No. There is no one else."

I hang up. I can't process this. I call Ellen who is going with me to Italy. She is always measured and calm and rational.

"Listen, I think he is just busy at work. He *will* call you this weekend. Just stay calm."

"No, no. He won't. He told Antonio he can't deal, that he is overwhelmed."

I exhale smoke.

"Okay, relax."

"I can't believe this. This is so weird. I'm not going to Italy."

"Yes, you are. Listen, forget him. You bought a ticket. You can stay with me and Daniel. You are going. We want you to go."

"Daniel's sister is coming! There is no room for me. And I am not imposing on you."

"You can stay with us. There is a pull-out sofa. Just stay with us."

I refuse. I do what my Dad always said to do. I book a hotel. I am going to Italy. Everyone, even including my skeptical parents and sister, say I should go.

"You love Italy. You have been working so hard lately. *Go!* Forget him. Go have fun with Daniel and Ellen. Go enjoy your life. You need to get away," my mom tells me.

I can't decide what to do. I'm in. I'm out. I'm up. I'm down. I book a hotel. I cancel a hotel. I check my messages, but he never writes. I smoke. I stop eating. I'm losing my mind for a guy all over again. I know it, but I can't stop it.

Finally, Daniel calls.

"Listen, you have to come. It's okay. It's okay if he hasn't called. He will. And you guys will work this all out in Italy. You just need to talk in person."

"I know. But he hasn't called Daniel."

"He will. I think he is just overwhelmed with work. Just come. You guys will work it out when you get there. Trust me. Trust me."

Everyone thinks he loves me. Everyone thinks it is somehow going to be okay once I get there.

Daniel sends me links to hotels just down the street from his house in Todi. The last thing I want to do is burden them. I finally firmly book a hotel, just like that. He's right. Fuck him. He doesn't own the country, and I'm going. I convince myself that I can have a good time without him.

So now it's Sunday night, and I still haven't heard from him.

I'm not going to hear from him. He's not going to pick me up from Rome. Daniel will. He says he will be waiting for me there.

My friends are proud that I'm going. They realize it's going to be hard, but they think I am strong. I am not strong. Everyone thinks that because I hide a lot of things from people. But I am the weakest of women. I am mentally weak. I don't know how I'm going to do this.

My friend Anna, who constantly advises me calls.

"I am proud of you for going. I couldn't do it. But please, please don't see him. Please don't contact him. Just enjoy yourself in Italy. Don't see him."

I get it. I mean, really. Do my friends really think my self-esteem is that low? Do they think I'm going to call him? Sleep with him? Come on. I do have some shred of dignity left.

I still hear nothing.

I pack my bag. I finally cave. I email him. I know he will read it.

Dear Fernando, I haven't heard from you. I have called and texted. I have no idea where you are or what is going on. If you are depressed or if you are overwhelmed, I understand. You could have just told me. I feel that we both have put too much pressure on this. On this trip. On talking about the future. I don't want to talk about the future. I know there are insurmountable obstacles. I don't want to move to Terni, and you likely won't be able to come here. I really wanted to have fun and have laughs—to smoke, drink and fuck again and not think about next week. And if this isn't what you wanted... you should have just told me. I gave you every fucking chance. You chose to not deal with it. You are a coward. You have disappointed me gravely. But I am coming to Todi and staying with Doug and Ellen. I will have Thanksgiving with my friends. And you do want you want. Enjoy your holiday.

He doesn't write back. He is crazy, and he is making me crazy.

Chapter Eleven

My dad drives me to the airport in the early morning. He knows what has happened. But we do not discuss it. Later, he will tell me he tried to discuss it with me, but I wouldn't talk. It is possible. I do not remember. My head is pressed against the windowpane the whole time. I am looking at snow cascading down rapidly and a gray sky and a Dunkin Donuts sign passes by. My dad asks if I want to stop for a jellyroll, and I simply say no and close my eyes.

And as I fly 11 hours to Rome, I start to feel okay again. I'm getting stronger. I have a glass of wine. Then another. I take a sleeping pill, but I can't sleep. I know he isn't going to be there when I arrive. I am 95 percent sure of this. But there is the five percent of me that is hoping, expecting that when I walk through Customs, he will be there. That this is all just a very bad dream.

As I go through Customs, trying to stay strong and resolved, Ellen texts me. She and Daniel are waiting for me at a café. I show the officials my passport. I gather my luggage. I walk out the big green door and turn left looking, hoping.

Fernando is not there.

It is all true. This is your life. Not some bad dream.

But Daniel is there. He is with Ellen and his sister having a cappuccino. They hug me, tell me it is okay. We will go to Rome today, and we will have fun.

"I need to get a coffee, okay? I am so tired."

I order an espresso at the airport café. The man who hands it to me says, *"Tu es belissima*! You are beautiful!"

"Fuck off. Just leave me alone. This is what got me in trouble in the first place."

And I mean it. I do not want to hear those meaningless words ever again. These Italian men— such a bunch of phonies. A bunch of mama's boys. Fuck them.

We spend the first day in Rome. And we do it all again. The Trevi Fountain. The Coliseum. But I don't care about Rome anymore.

Ellen and I are just ugly Americans. We just want to shop and shop a lot. Actually, one could argue the second part of the story should be titled *Smoke Drink Shop* because that is pretty much all we did the entire time.

We leave Daniel and his anal-retentive uber intellectual sister. I am in no mood to be cerebral and a historian in Rome. We slither down narrow alleys with big open windows revealing lots of cool shit that happens to be on sale. We buy amazing camel cashmere sweaters and black dresses and oversized leather belts. The sister wants to look at the architecture and the real beauty of Rome, and Ellen and I are all about the fashion. I am starting to think I really am Jackie O. I only want to buy my clothes and handbags in Italy now. I decide I am going to do this once a year and load up.

And I post everything on Facebook because I know he is reading my status updates. That lame addictive Facebook is the only place where we are still consummately connected. Ellen and I take shitloads of photos, and we deliberately include lots of random men in them. Some strapping young lad policeman types hug us on the Spanish Steps. We post those too.

I look like I am the happiest girl in the world. My hair is perfect as it has just been professionally styled. I have on all brand new clothes that I bought right before the trip. I'm thinner than I've ever been. I joyously toss a coin behind my head into the Trevi Fountain making a real wish this time that won't come true.

I look like I am having a fucking blast in Rome.

We go to an amazing restaurant for lunch, one Daniel has been to many times before. He speaks Italian, has an Italian passport. He is now more Italian than American.

Ellen and I order super-fattening Spaghetti Carbonara. And fried artichokes. And antipasti.

But I cannot eat. I have no appetite. I already lost eight pounds before I even arrived without even stepping a foot into the gym. I pick at all the food. Ellen has already downed a fried artichoke heart, chickpeas, rocket salad, prosciutto, pecorino. She is all about the meals. And she is rail thin. I just want to smoke and go to my hotel and be alone. As I down the Prosecco, I feel the overwhelming sadness. It's getting hard to hold all this inside.

At lunch, the topic comes up again. We discuss it.

We analyze it. Daniel is still in shock that Fernando hasn't called, but I'm not. I know he won't. At times, the pain in my heart is totally overwhelming, but I won't let it show. I am determined to have a good time and not ruin the lives of others.

At 6:00, we drive the two hours to Todi.

When we arrive later that night, Daniel takes me back to my hotel. I am so jetlagged, but I cannot sleep. So I write. I write Fernando a letter, and I rewrite it. I tear up paper. I start again. I may never see him again, but I am going to say what I want to say here on this paper.

And finally, at midnight, I just lose it. I do the thing I never wanted to do. I cry and cry, and I can't stop crying. I feel like my eyeballs, the only organs are going to fall right out of my fucking head. I choke on my tears and can't stop coughing. I dry heave and collapse on my bed.

I think I may be having a nervous breakdown.

I feel like someone is ripping out my heart and my soul, and I really cannot bear to go on. I call my best friend George in the States. I dump it all on him, for at least 40 minutes. God knows how much this fucking call is going to cost me. God knows how much this fucker has put me back period.

I have no idea what time it is there.

George just listens. I can't breathe. I reach for my inhaler and take a deep breath. He tells me he feels awful and how all of this makes no sense. He tells me it will get better. He does what any good friend does. He just tries to talk me off the ledge. I take a Xanax. I'm living on Xanax. I collapse and sleep for a very very long time.

I wake up. Open my eyes to the gleaming sun creeping in through the sheer, white curtains. For more than a moment, I think I'm in Terni in Fernando's bed again, but he isn't there. And I don't hear the church bells or the pigeons this time.

I check my iPhone.

Nothing.

This is your life.

My hotel balcony faces many many beautiful rolling green and yellow meadows that are laced with vines on wire fences with little rock castles nestled in the middle of them. It looks just like it did last time. You wouldn't believe the view except I don't much look at it this time.

As the sun permeates the room, I keep going back in my mind to that moment in the early morning in his bedroom.

The morning's blinding white sun peeking in through long, tall white wooden shutter doors that are open and rocking back and forth from the light breeze. Creaking then a pause, then a creak again.

It is Sunday morning, and the church bells are going off every 15 minutes. Pigeons fly in a flock toward the top of the doors and rest at the top flapping their wings fervently. I am exhausted and barely opening my eyes.

I am in his bed, and we are starting to wake up. I'm lying on my back naked and wet wrapped in a thin white sheet, and he has one foot over my calf—lying on his stomach, head turned toward the doors, but holding my left hand tightly. My arm is raised and under his pillow. I don't remember how it got there, but I know we are never not touching the entire night.

He sees me open my eyes—the sun is so piercing. Immediately, he rolls over and toward me and just holds me tightly for a long time. I feel safe. I finally feel safe. They say you are supposed to feel safe with the person who you love. I never knew what that felt like until now.

It is just a dream. Wake up.

I go downstairs to the lobby where they serve a not so decent complimentary breakfast. I down three cappuccinos. I do not eat. I hate all the breakfast cookies and pastries. Who wants to eat little cookies for breakfast anyway? Who wants to eat period?

I flashback to last August in Terni.

I am in a black dress seated at a small round table at an outdoor café on a cobbled brick street having cappuccinos with him. He hands me pink and yellow and blue confettis on a small white porcelain plate.

"This is confetti. We have this for breakfast. We give this at weddings too. Here... here are some cookies for you."

"I do not eat cookies for breakfast." I smile. "Cookies... well, they are for after lunch. Chocolate chip cookies! And for breakfast, I prefer eggs."

I can't seem to stop flashing back.

Daniel and Ellen pick me up outside the hotel lobby in the drizzling rain. It gets dark at four in the winter, and this time, it's always cold and rainy. We go to the anachronistic Todi gym. Daniel is a regimented man, a creature of habit. He must work out every single day, and I figure it's better to join them than sit around in my mediocre hotel staring at cookies and having flashbacks. I don't know where I pull out

157

the energy to move. But I somehow manage to get on that crappy Medieval treadmill, and I run and run. I run until my lungs collapse. It helps. I have so much fucking anger that I think I will beat the treadmill. I can run longer and faster than it can. I can run a million miles or more.

The endorphins eventually convert into some form of serotonin. And I feel better for it afterwards. I'm really doing everything I can to make myself feel better besides perhaps drinking a kiloliter of red wine.

I shower. I do my hair—an endless process in and of itself. A low-grade Italian blow dryer. Three hair straightening products. A straightening iron. It's raining, and it is cold. There are no sunflowers. There are no wide-open green fields laden with golden bales of hay this time. There is no man with roses waiting for me outside.

I know this attempt at making myself look acceptable really is an exercise in futility, but I do it all nonetheless. I have to try. I slip on my new slimming, overpriced jeans and a new black cashmere sweater and black riding boots. That's the other thing. I have bought all these cute clothes for this trip, and he will never even see me in any of them. Such an asshole. I lost eight fucking pounds for these tight-as-hell, $250 jeans.

I want to stab him. In fact, I constantly think about stabbing him in his heart with a knife or fork… whatever I can find first in his restaurant.

I wish so much I had gone to his restaurant yesterday and thrown a huge glass of red wine over his crisp, white probably Tom Ford shirt and ruined it. I would have called him a coward and a liar and just left. At least then, at that moment, he would have been held accountable and had to face me. However—and perhaps this explains things a bit—there is no word in Italian for "accountability." The closest thing really is *responsabilita,* which means responsibility.

And if I had done it, I wouldn't have even looked psycho. I mean, these Italians are so passionate and dramatic, the ladies would have been like, "Oh, just another Tuesday here."

I go over it and over with Daniel.

"Daniel, he is here. He is literally 20 miles away. How can I not go there? I deserve an explanation. Don't I deserve I explanation?"

"You can't go to the restaurant, Esme."

"I know. I just can't believe this. I don't want to cause drama. I don't. I just want to know why."

"There is no explanation. He's crazy. The guy has serious mental issues. Truly, you are better off without him. How would you feel if this happened in Portugal?"

"I just want to go to the restaurant for ten minutes just to see him and make him face me."

"I'll take you if you really want to go, but I don't think you should. I'll wait in the car for you for ten minutes. That's it."

"Don't go, Esme. Come on. You can't do this. You can't let him see you this way." Ellen takes my hand. She is all about dignity and pride.

I see her point.

"Okay. Okay. I won't go."

I resign myself to the fact that I will never know. I will never see him again.

The next day Daniel drives us to the nearby town

of Orvietto to shop and have some fun. I mean seriously, Todi really only has so much to offer. The city has all of about six streets, and I covered *it all the first time.* And our favorite jewelry store is closed all the time for the *"riposso."* These people sure do nap a lot.

In Orvietto, Daniel and his sister want to explore the chapels and cathedrals. Daniel and the sister are meaningful, deep people who have the foundation of religion in their lives. I am empty and vacuous and a non-practicing nothing. I am just desperately searching for something to make me feel better immediately. Ellen, to my good fortune, is Jewish (and a princess, to boot) and rejects anything Catholic. She embraces our shared interest in shallow secular activities. *Allora!*

At this point, it's going to be either a big fucking glass of vino rosso or a big Roman sweater.

I know this kind of sounds just like part one of the book, but this time it's a lot worse. Nihilistic. Shallow. Self destructive. Worse than I was before if that is even possible. I spend a lot more money this time.

And I don't really care how you label it. Don't judge me. You'd do the same thing. There is no fucking way stained glass windows or crucifixes are going to make me feel better now. And I ain't lighting a candle for St. Peter. I already told you I have prayed *a lot,* and it hasn't worked. At all.

We don't have a lot of time to shop though. Daniel wants to go somewhere else and soon. I feel programmed. Rushed. Distinct reminder of my days with Mr. Roboto. I long for those luxurious lunches of last August. Fernando never rushed me—he told me to take as long as I needed, and when I was ready, we would go home.

We first drive 30 miles to a quaint castle in the middle of a wet grassy field, up a winding road covered with broken white stones. It is where Daniel's daughter soon will be married. It is the most romantic place I have seen in my life. He and the sister want to meet with people, see rooms, visit yet another chapel and take pictures.

This is exactly the place I could have seen Fernando and I getting married one day. I remember him saying that if I was in Terni, we would be engaged. Why not get not married here?

It is so beautiful. It is so fucking depressing. I do not want to see any more of this place—that's for sure. And I certainly do not want to take any pictures. Ellen doesn't really want to either. She and Daniel are always a nanosecond away from breaking up because she wants to adopt a baby and he doesn't, and we both know that we're probably not going to be invited to the wedding anyway.

Thank God for Ellen because she is as not into this shit as I am. I have a companion in my self-induced misery. We bolt. We find a bar in the stable. We order one Prosecco and then another.

And we just talk and talk. We talk about her relationship with Daniel. Her desire to adopt a baby and his lack of interest in it. We talk about our hellish work schedules and our deep regret for putting so much emphasis on our careers over the past 20 years. Then, we get to Fernando's unbelievable disappearing act.

But Ellen really isn't making me feel better. She has no explanation or solid advice on this mater.

"Do you think he will ever call me? I mean, God! I'm in his fucking country. Is he really not going to talk to me ever again? Ever?"

"I don't think you're going to hear from him."

Always honest. Always the pragmatist. She calmly sips her Prosecco and looks out the side window.

"Are you serious?"

"Listen. I just think he is off the radar. Just off of it. I mean clearly, he has mental issues. Clearly, he is fucked up from his father. Come on. You know this."

"Don't you feel sorry for me? Come on. Just a little bit sorry for me?"

I squint my eyes. Surely, she must feel some empathy, right? I mean this is quite a mindfuck.

She gives me this half smile. Not the sensitive warm embrace I was searching for.

"Ugh," she shrugs her shoulders. "No, in a way I don't. I mean he's crazy. You are better off without him. So much better off. I think you managed to dodge a big bullet."

And just then, I start cracking up and spit my Prosecco all over the table.

"You are such a bitch! That half smile! I cannot believe you. You don't even feel sorry for me. You are *so so* not giving me the answer I want, Ellen."

"Well," she is laughing now at me. "I just think you are so much better off without him. And better you found out *now.* Truly. What if you had gone to Portugal with him and he pulled this shit?"

She is right. He could have pulled this freakout shit in Portugal. And there I would be, stuck in Lisbon in a hotel he paid for. He would have the plane tickets.

162

I mean, I'm sure I would have somehow found my way to the Lisbon airport, but she is right. This could have been far, far worse.

We drive home, and the four of us make a half-American/half-Italian Thanksgiving dinner. The dinner that Fernando said he would prepare for all us. I had cancelled our extended invitations without any explanation. There was none. Each of us will make one dish. I, cooking challenged, make the caprese. The only think I can make and the only thing I ever want to eat anyway.

I check Facebook. All the time. It is our only connection.

He is constantly posting in English now (he always posts in Italian) macabre disturbing things that he knows I will read.

At times like this... I need to escape.

Perhaps I will never come back.

Then in Italian (Here is the English translation):

At times like this, I lie in bed, turning my balls, and I wish I could watch the sunset with my mother or with "a" woman I love. I get emotional. But I know I must be alone. I must sleep alone.

I show this one to Daniel, who speaks fluent Italian.

"What in the hell does this mean? This ball turning thing?"

He grabs my iPhone.

"I don't know. I mean the words literally mean turning my testicles."

"Do you guys do that? Do you just turn them around... like twank, twank?"

He and Ellen laugh.

"No. No. We don't do that. It must mean something different in Italian."

"Ask Stefano."

Stefano is the meathead electrician next-door neighbor who Daniel has a man-crush on. We frequently remind him of this. It's like he'd rather talk (in Italian—no English with Stefano) to this boorish man all night rather than the brilliant men he works with on a daily basis in DC. Well, who am I to judge? I talk all night long to some random chef in Italy who has no idea what my daily life is like and has no knowledge of business or government or anything in the real world. Sometimes it is just easier and more pleasant to talk about tomatoes than health care reform or the state of things in Egypt.

"No. I am not going to call him. Come on."

"Listen up! I want to know what it means. Just call him. I can't speak Italian!"

"You have to call him. Come on. We need to know what it means."

Ellen coaxes him.

Daniel finally capitulates and calls Stefano. I hear them speaking rapidly in Italian and Daniel laughing.

"Okay guys, according to Stefano, this whole balls turning thing means you are annoyed or angry or in some of an emotional state. But Stefano said this is not an appropriate thing to post on Facebook. It's kind of crass."

We laugh out loud. There is a moment of respite from the grief.

But seriously, come on. After all this shit he has pulled, he *is* angry? Annoyed? The narcissism is truly unbelievable.

After the balls-turning post, I call Antonio, who is

flying in soon with Bridget to have Thanksgiving dinner with the sociopath.

"Listen, I'm not a psychiatrist. You are. But these postings he is constantly putting up are really disturbing. I'm worried about him. You need to call him."

"I will call him, I will call him," he assures me. "We will have dinner with him tonight. I get in at seven, and we will come to Daniel's after that to see you. Don't worry."

And so he calls him. And still there is no explanation.

We eat dinner. I don't eat the turkey or the cobbler or the zucchini casserole. I just pound the wine. I plan on knocking myself out.

Daniel and Ellen are tense and arguing often. He is annoyed at us because he feels he is just driving us around so we can shop—which may be true. He also doesn't like that we want to go to the Todi spa tomorrow and get a massage and go to the wine tasting. I refuse to be intellectual or substantive on this trip. I want to get a massage, smoke, drink wine(s), and buy another sweater. Give me what I want! Why is this so wrong? Umbria is pretty chill. There's not a lot to do here. Might as well buy some sweaters or eat some truffles. Not much else going on, Daniel.

"Let's just get drunk." Ellen grabs my arm and pours more red.

Antonio and Bridget arrive at 10:00 p.m. They are kind and gracious. They bring us a bottle of red wine from the nearby Montefalco region and a bottle of hand-pressed olive oil. They all talk. I don't hear anything at all.

I feel rushed to get Antonio alone in a room. I need to know what Fernando said.

"Antonio, I need a cigarette. Will you come with me to the patio?"

"Yes, of course." He follows me out to the patio.

"Antonio, Antonio. What is going on? Just tell me. Just please tell me the truth. Did he meet someone else? Just tell me. Tell me please what is going on."

"I didn't see him. I didn't have dinner with him.

"What are you talking about? I thought you guys were having dinner with him tonight?"

"That was the plan but... "

"But what? Where is he?"

"He has left. He has left the country."

"What are you talking about?"

"I called him. I did, after you saw all that weird stuff he posted on Facebook. He told me he was overwhelmed. Unhappy. He said he was going to leave. He was going to go to Istanbul or Cairo."

"WHAT?"

"I think he's in Istanbul, but he won't answer his phone."

"Istanbul? Are you fucking kidding me?"

I've been to Istanbul. It is not a place you "escape" to. Istanbul is overwhelming, okay? I mean if you want to escape, go to the south of France. Go to fucking St. Tropez. I cannot believe this.

"I know. I know. I'm sorry. I don't know what to say. I'm very disappointed in him."

"What is going on? Just tell me. I don't care what it is. Just tell me. Did he meet someone else?"

I keep thinking this must be it. This is what happens when guys disappear. And at least I will now know the truth.

"No. No. There is no one else. He just told me he

is overwhelmed and could not cope—that he needed to escape."

"Okay, okay. Listen, I'm sorry to drag you into all this."

"It is not a bother. Don't worry. Honestly, I was quite embarrassed by his behavior. I was embarrassed to even come over here. But you know, he has attachment issues. He didn't have a good role model. His father left him when he was young."

I have heard it all before.

"We will pick you up in the morning. We will all go to Spoleto. It will be a nice day."

He kisses my cheeks. He is so calm. I want to shake him.

Now I am going to travel Italy with *his* friends. I mean, this is just too weird.

Well, why not? They like me better anyway.

Fuck him.

The next day, Daniel calls me at the hotel and says he is picking me up and we will be meeting Bridget and Antonio in Narni.

Narni? Where the hell is this place? What happened to Spoleto and shopping? I want to go to Spoleto!

"Narni?" I question Daniel as I climb in the back seat.

"Are you kidding me? I thought we were going to Spoleto."

Narni is a little town south of Terni that is basically a dump. There are all these lovely charming towns in fucking Umbria, and this is where they pick? And industrial wasteland. There are stone buildings and more cobblestone streets; it is famous for the largest Roman bridge (big deal). C.S. Lewis's imaginary land of Narnia was supposedly named after Narni after he came across the name in an atlas as a child. Trust me. There is nothing magical about Narni.

How in the hell did this plan change without consulting me and Ellen? We do *not* want to go to some other allegedly quaint village and look at more freaking chapels and broken Roman bridges from the 13th Century.

We want to smoke, drink and shop.

SDS!!

"Antonio called this morning. He changed his mind. He wants to show us this town."

Daniel states this fact firmly. I can tell we are really annoying him with our complete lack of cultural interest.

Shit. Now I'm really in for it. I might as well pray. Or eat a lot. I might as well turn into fucking Liz Gilbert now. There is nothing else to do in Narni but worship. I just know it.

And I'm so right about that. Antonio, a cerebral Italian doctor so proud of his country, is our tour guide. He takes us slowly up the cobblestone road of nothingness—broken bridges, half-blown out Roman arches, and ruins. Rain is drizzling, and it is gray and cold, almost dark. This is not the warm green and yellow Italy I remember—holding hands with Fernando and driving through fields of sunflowers. This looks like fucking Warsaw.

I've seen my share of ruins. Hell, I have a ruined soul inside. I just want to have some fun! Geez. Why does everything here have to be a history lesson? I got all this in Latin class, and I slept through most of that.

I constantly wish Fernando would just appear and whisk me off to Arroni. He'd be a lot of fun. I'd make him take me to Spoleto and show me a good time. I'm not kidding you. I have to get out of industrial war-torn Narni.

And then the chapels... They go into three of them and learn all about them. I do not light a candle for someone dead as Daniel does. I do look at the stained-glass windows. It reminds of the chapel I was in with Fernando in Orvietto, and now I'm getting depressed again missing him. I cannot focus. I just want out of this church. I feel my chest closing up. I reach for my inhaler. And then a smoke.

It is almost 3:00 at this point, and I am freezing. I pull Ellen aside and light up a smoke.

"Listen," I whisper. "I'm about done with the Roman ruins, okay? I know, I know. They are into it. I am an ugly American that just wants to drink and shop. I'm depressed because Fernando has absconded to Turkey or maybe Egypt. Okay, I admit it. But I need to get out of here."

She laughs.

"No, I'm serious," I whisper in her ear. "Listen, I know Daniel is into all this shit, but I can't go into one more chapel. I really can't. And it's okay... we all want different things out of a trip. I am going to slip out and go shop. You can meet me there later. *Ciao!*"

I start to take off.

She laughs and grabs my elbow.

"Wait. I want to shop too... but I don't think the stores open till like 4:00. You know, the *riposo.*"

"Oh, yeah. That fucking *riposo.* I can never buy what I want when I want it because all these people sleep during the day."

"Let's just go with Antonio a little bit longer, and then we'll split."

Ellen the consummate princess pretending to be conciliatory and accommodating. She found a great time to start this act.

I acquiesce.

"But I really need a cocktail. And we need more sweaters."

It goes on and on. I complain to Bridget. She agrees this Roman tour must end.

"I'm with you. I just want a fag and a drink."

Finally, the fucking tour ends. But of course, it is now pitch black, and quite honestly, not surprisingly, there are shit shops in Narni. Tire stores. Gray smokestacks. Empty buildings.

So we don't shop. And by now everyone is hungry and wants to relax. Except me. I can't sit still. I just want to move around and avoid what's going on in my head. If I sit, I will think. I will miss Fernando. I will think of the last time I was here. I will get depressed. I don't want to get depressed. And why in fuck do these people have to eat constantly? I have no appetite. I just can't eat this much. I have Drunkarexia. Let's just rip open the champagne and start drinking so I can go numb.

I mean, I love the Italians, but seriously, all they talk about is food and wine. They could spend 30 minutes just describing the type of olive oil they use. And by the way, they are about ready to get kicked out of the G-8 and have 29% youth unemployment. I don't think as an American woman there is one thing I could do here for a living other than sleep in Berlusconi's bed. The Italians really need to stop obsessing about the Pecorino and Parma and develop a microprocessor or green technology. I mean, really: Are gelato shops and tabaccheri stores really going to sustain their economy?

We go for aperitif. Charcutterie platter—Parma, pecorino, asiago, speck, prosciutto, salami, bread, olives, pistachios, liver, tomatoes, and black-olive bruschetta. And this is an appetizer?

The waiter pops open the Prosecco. I'm all about the cocktails. But as I look at the black-and-white Picasso sketches on the stark white walls, all the thoughts of Fernando start to race through my mind. I want the fuck out of gray industrial Narni. I might as well be in Detroit.

* * *

After two drinks, Daniel tells me he is tired. It's only 7:00. He wants to get back for an early dinner in Todi at Sylvia and Pierro's, the local joint next to his house. No. Not. I've already eaten there half a dozen times, and I'm sick of it and those country bumpkins in Todi. Ellen looks at me longingly. She so wants to stay with me and go out and party. The sister sides with him. They are out of here. I often wish I was the type of person who didn't crave excitement but preferred ritual and going to bed early. Life would be so much easier then.

"Esme, just stay with us. We're going to go out in Terni. We'll meet up with my friend Francesca for dinner. She lives in Perugia. She will drive you home, or I will," Antonio offers.

Bridget clenches my hand. "Let's go have a fag and a cocktail."

Allora! The partiers are in the house. I'm so not going back to boring Todi.

"I'm going to stay with Antonio and Bridget, I think. Are you okay with that?"

I whisper to Ellen.

"Yes. Yes. Stay. We're going to go home. Daniel is tired."

"Okay. I'll see you tomorrow. Ciao, bella."

We kiss cheeks. Finally, I am rid of the cerebrals. Let's get this party started!

Bridget and I walk ahead of Antonio.

"Time for cocktails!"

She grabs my arm. We are kindred spirits. Looking to have some fun.

Antonio catches up, and we are walking the busy brick street of Terni where I spent many many hours with Fernando. It all comes back to me.

"I want to walk by the restaurant, Antonio."

I suddenly grab his arm.

"I want to make sure it is closed. I don't believe him. He may not even be in Istanbul."

"Okay, okay." He indulges me. "Here it is, to the left."

The white awning is there, absent the patio tables we sat under in the early evening sun. The lights are off in the yellow brick building. The restaurant is closed. Fernando really is gone.

"Okay. Let's go."

"Are you okay?" Bridget grabs my elbow.

"Yes. I'm fine."

I manage to pull it together. He will not break me.

I have the letter I have written to him with me. I think of slipping it under the door. I think about knocking on the door to make sure he really isn't in there. I think about doing a million things, but I do nothing.

"Esme, this place is very good. Very good."

Antonio points down the street to the left.

"We will go here and have champagne, and then we will go meet Francesca for dinner."

I don't care where the fuck we go. Just get me away from his restaurant. I can't ever go back there.

We approach a small rowhouse with a white brick exterior bordered by a large white awning and cobalt blue letters—Placebo. We sit in the back at a small pine table, and Antonio orders an expensive bottle of French pink champagne. I speak to the waitress in Italian. I've been studying it because Fernando asked me to, and I am picking it up faster now that I'm here. I learned a whole language for the jackass. All those Rosetta Stone CDs and all those Italian podcasts on my iPod that I'd listen to every night at the gym. What a stupid girl. What a waste of time. I should have fallen for a Chinese man. At least learning Mandarin could be added to my Linked In Profile as a valuable skill.

However, as I sit here with the champagne relaxing and speaking the language I managed to learn, I start to fall in love with Italy all over again. It is in me because it is the lifestyle I believe in and consistently choose not to live in the U.S. In Italy, life is all about family, conversation, good friends, and eating and drinking. Sign me up. Work, which has dominated my entire existence for nearly 20 years is overrated. I'm sick of trying to have a perfect resume and having to add more and more

173

skill sets, apps, and languages. I'm tired of just "applying" for jobs, board positions and writing competitions. Who really cares? Who really wants to be an SVP and have a country club membership? Would you really meet interesting people there?

I know I could move here tomorrow and be very happy (if I could just find something to do for a living). Fernando hates Terni and makes fun of Umbria and the "simple-minded, boring people" that live here. But for me, this really is better than anything America has to offer. I'll even take Stefano, the meatball electrician. I'll take the simple minded. I'm so sick of the pretentious people who just want to suck you for your contacts and connections... the kind of people that I have been dealing with for the last decade. And I'm sick of networking. I don't even have the energy anymore to meet someone "new."

So we have some pink champagne. I feel better. I immediately connect with the bubbles.

Bridget stands up.

"I'm going to get some food. I'll be right back."

There is an enormous amount of happy hour food here—lentils, fava beans, pasta, bruschetta, speck, salami. Good God. How do these people eat so much and so often? I just downed a cow and a pig a half an hour ago.

Antonio joins her for some *lenticias*. I just pound the champagne. No need to eat. I'm not going to put on eight pounds for some guy. I'll have a proper liquid diet and an occasional slab of pork.

Bridget and Antonio partake in Aperitif numero duo. I excuse myself to have a smoke.

"I'll come with you!" Bridget smiles. "Antonio doesn't like it when I smoke, but we're on holiday so..."

"Oh, fuck them. They always hate when we smoke. Whatever."

Except Fernando didn't care at all when I smoked. He didn't care what I did. I think I could have had sex with a goat on his kitchen table right in front of him and he would have just shrugged his shoulders and smiled. He probably would have found it charming. He seemed to think anything I did was totally charming.

As we enter the blistering cold in some degrees of Celsius that I do not understand, Bridget lights her cigarette off mine and says,

"Listen, I'm so sorry. I really am. I have no idea what happened."

My stomach sinks. Oh God. We're back to him. I can't seem to stop talking about him. It's really exhausting me, and it's my own story. It must be incredibly exhausting to them. That mental patient has somehow managed to be present at every step of this trip even though he's likely smoking a hookah pipe with unbridled glee right now somewhere in fucking Turkey.

"It's not your fault. Please. But tell me, just tell me… has he always been this crazy?"

I keep looking back. Over and over. What did I miss? Why didn't I see the train wreck coming? How could I have not known that he was a fucking sociopath not this amazing man I somehow created?

* * *

I think back to that morning in Orvietto when Jackie and Fabio were in the cathedral, and we sat together on the stairs. He suddenly said nothing. He

175

seemed sad, withdrawn. He changed a bit. I felt like I couldn't reach him. I remember feeling my stomach sinking a bit because I felt something was wrong, but then I stopped, I told myself I was overanalyzing things as usual…

After a few hours of touring chapels ended, and lunchtime was creeping up on us. Jackie and I pointed to a restaurant where we wanted to stop for lunch.

"No, no darling, follow me, I know the perfect place."

He took me by the hand, and we all walked over cobblestone streets with Byzantine turns. I had no idea where we were or where we were going. I just wanted a drink and to stop walking. And I wanted him to start acting doting and attentive again.

"Here, here it is."

We approached a quaint restaurant with a lemon-yellow awning with six or seven pine wood tables pressed close together. There was a bar on the side of the tables stocked full of wine, Limoncello, and a red cappuccino maker.

"Yes, this is the place. This place is very nice. Very nice. Trust me," Fabio assured us.

Fernando immediately ordered two bottles of Pinot Grigio. He didn't even look at the wine list.

As we started drinking wine, he came alive again. We joked. We made fun of Fabio. He ordered all the food he wanted us to try. Antipasto with red rolled-up meats and hard yellow cheeses. Then rocket salads with shaved Parma. Veal drenched in brown sauce and porcini mushrooms. Spaghetti Carbonara with eggs and bacon drizzled on top.

Fresh cantaloupe and prosciutto. Little shots of

Limoncello. We ate. We drank. We laughed. As always, he encouraged me over and over to eat more.

After lunch, as the four of us exited the restaurant, he darted across the street.

"Where are you going? Fernando!"

"I'll be back. Don't worry."

He came back with little chocolates, which he gave to Jackie. Then he handed me tiny pink and sky-blue and white circles of sugar.

I pushed them away.

"I am not hungry. I do not want any now."

"Take them with you then." He opened my hand, pushed in the tablets, then closed it.

"Okay, okay." I shoved them in my purse.

When I got back home, I placed the circular plastic box with the sugars on my desk and rubbed them from time to time. Creating a vision board. Putting it all out into the universe.

Fuck those sugars. I threw them away last week. I hope they're rotting now in some dump in New Jersey.

But I guess when I look back on it now, there were some signs. That day the sudden shift in his personality. The extreme and sudden quietness. Cutting Fabio out of his life after one minor argument over proper restaurant etiquette. The extreme anger over Fabio's comments on my Facebook wall. The strange talk of going to Holland with Allejandro to try and find his missing father. There were weird things. I think I just ignored them all because I thought he was this amazing man, and I wanted to believe everything was true, just as we planned.

* * *

During this entire trip though, Antonio's fiancée, Bridget, is so kind and so sympathetic. I actually couldn't ask for a better travel companion during my on-autopilot-almost-psychotic states. Bridget is a psycho-pharmacologist who deals daily with personality disorders. She has suffered from depression herself but sees hope in her patients. She loves to drink and smoke. Bridget rocks. She was amazing throughout it, and this certainly wasn't her problem to deal with.

"I'm so very sorry, Esme. I honestly can't believe this. We never saw it coming either."

"There is no explanation. I don't know…"

I smoke my cigarette and check out of the conversation by turning my head toward an empty alley.

"I still can't believe it. I just can't believe this happened." Bridget continues.

"He has a personality disorder. Trust me. I deal with these people all day. I dealt with a woman last week who was putting mercury into her own breasts because she was paranoid someone was taking over her body. She gave herself cancer."

"Oh, my God. I have no idea how you guys deal with this."

"It's hard. But they get better. People do get better."

"Will Fernando ever get better?"

"It isn't likely." She inhales and turns away.

"Why not?"

I think maybe we just need some good old American meds. I keep thinking if I call my friend Gianna, a Pfizer pharmaceutical rep specializing in mental disorders, that she can ship over some Pristiq for my depression and some Geodon for his bipolar personality, and we can maybe get this thing back on track.

"There really isn't medication for it. It's all about their childhood. They need psychotherapy. Many years of it." She exhales.

"But most of them will just never get it. Certainly not Italian men."

It hits me. Fuck. There is no cure for this man. There is not a pill, as I had hoped. Come on. What manic, fucked-up guy is going to sign up for six years of psychotherapy in the hope that he someday can get into a normal relationship? Please.

We smoke. We drink. I wish I could fuck, but I can't. And in the alternative, I wish I could shop, but the shops are all closed now.

We rush back into the restaurant, find Antonio and pound some more champagne, and then we are off to round three of dinner with Francesca.

Chapter Twelve

Antonio is Jesus. Bridget is Mary. They are my saviors. They are *his* friends whom I have run to and absconded with. I've taken them as my own. They have picked me up and taken me with them and showed me new things. They have been there to listen to me each and everyday. They have even tried to fix things between us. They have gotten me through this.

We rush, scratchy wool scarves in tow, to the next place. Antonio seats us, hangs up our coats—a perfect gentleman—then rushes back to the cold street to park Francesca's car. Francesca is Antonio's friend and classmate from medical school in Perugia. I do not want to meet her. I do not want to know her. I do not want to tell the story again or hear it one more time.

But then she arrives. She is amazing. Yet another one of those Sophia Loren/Isabella Rossellini types you find all over Italy.

Shiny silky black hair in a perfectly cropped, angled bob. Olive skin and makeup that is sparkly and plum and perfect. Thick white quilted coat draped with a shiny black bowling-bag purse. She slips off her coat and tosses back her hair. She has on a simple but sexy long black dress with high-heeled patent leather boots, a deep purple shoulder sweater hangs loosely over her shoulders. She laughs out loud. She is confident. Full of life. She is a doctor in Italy *and* Sweden to boot. I want to be her.

We order red wine. We order more fucking charcuterie platters. Enough with the meat and cheese.

And then we confront the white elephant (not present) at the table—Fernando.

"What? What?" She shrieks and slams down her glass of wine turning to Antonio.

"He didn't pick her up from the Rome airport? He didn't pick her up? This girl... this beautiful girl... who has literally crossed oceans to see him? There is not excuse for this. No excuse!"

Antonio shrugs and puts his arms in the air.

"I know. I know. We are very disappointed."

"Disappointed? That's what you have to say for your friend's behavior?"

He gapes at her.

"Listen," she turns to me. "I don't know Fernando that well. I only met him once. I think it was a few weeks after you left. He was in Perugia with Antonio, and I met them for drinks with some friends. He talked about you nonstop! He told me he was in love and moving to the States and was going to be with you. He went on and on. I mean, I don't even know you—but I felt like I knew you before I even came out tonight."

"I never told him to move to America. That was all him. Trust me."

"I believe you. Antonio! Come on! This guy is your friend, and you are going to let him get away with this? No! No!"

181

She slams her wine glass down again.

"As a doctor, I will tell you... he has major issues. He has demons in his head. But that doesn't matter. He is an adult! He cannot run away from his problems like a child does! He has to face this! He has to be accountable. Come on, Antonio, come on! You need to talk to him."

"I agree. I will talk to him when I see him."

"Talk to him? You will get him to pay this poor girl's expenses! He will pay for them. She is a solicitor. You have to send him a letter, on your legal stationery!"

"I am not going to do that it. I don't even practice anymore. As if he would care! Forget it."

"No, you must! You must do it. Not for the money, but for the accountability! He must learn! Actions have consequences. You cannot just run and hide. He is not a bambino anymore. He is an adult. No. No."

She shakes her head and sips her wine.

"I agree. You are solicitor. You could write it," Antonio chimes in.

"Come on. And write what? I don't even practice law anymore."

"Tell him that either he pays your expenses, or he will never be able to get into the U.S. again! He will believe it," Antonio continues.

Francesca nods in agreement.

"Please. Please. You have to do it! Antonio, I will make you tell him this when you see him in December. I will email you. I will hound you. You must make him pay!"

Wow. She is *way* stronger than the American

girls I know. She immediately goes for the one place a man cares about: the wallet. She is the type of woman I want to be—strong, confident, no nonsense tolerated. Around her, I feel insecure and uncertain and neurotic. She seems comfortable alone, moving back to Sweden to do medical research and one who would have seen the signs.

"And you must write about this. I have had many international romances. One just recently with a guy in New York City." She imitates him: "Move here, move here. I want to be with you. And then he disappears!"

"Write about this," she laughs. "Clearly, this is an international problem."

I think about my friend Alessandra telling me about how the men she dates are ghosts—always disappearing. I think, in a self-absorbed fashion, that this is a unique phenomenon. It's never happened to me before, at least not quite like this. But perhaps it is more pervasive than I think. And perhaps there is nothing that can be done. And perhaps you will never have the answer you are looking for. You will just have to embrace the ambiguity and somehow in some way *let it go.*

Bridget leans forward toward me.

"Yes. Write about this situation. I know I am lucky to have met Antonio. But we moved quickly too. You can't beat yourself up about it. On our third date, he took me to Paris. On the fourth date, we moved in together, and we've been together ever since. You just never know."

Exactly. Bridget and Antonio moved at record pace, and in two months they will get married. No one judges the people for whom it all works out. For them, moving fast and intensely is only evidence of love at first sight. *But everyone judges people like me for moving too fast—the people for whom it doesn't work out.*

The next night, my last night, we go to a tall stone castle hidden in the middle of Umbria.

Antonio found it for us. It is now a hotel and quaint *ristorante.*

Daniel, his sister, Ellen, Bridget and Antonio and I eat and eat. I'm finally eating like the Italians do. I'm feeling better.

Salami, prosciutto, speck, pecorino, Parma and then pasta and veal and more and more vino rossi. I don't think I can move. Bridget and I are out of smokes. We panic. But the restaurant is starting to close up, and in Italy, they let you smoke inside. Excellent.

We are tipsy and obnoxious and see a couple seated way in the back smoking.

We walk right up to them and apologetically ask for smokes. They invite us to sit with them. The woman has long, sleek carrot-topped hair, funky black glasses, a hip horizontal striped sweater, and black leggings. She is so beautiful and confident. She looks like the women you see riding motorcycles in Indie films.

"No worries," she says, and hands us a cigarette. "I'm Cris, Esme."

Her boyfriend, Romeo is all curly black hair and olive skin and smoking and smiles. I will later learn they are on their first date.

"What brings you to Italy?" she asks.

Bridget replies first.

"Well, I'm British but my fiancée is Italian and from here, so we're here for the holidays. And she is American and came here to see the man she loves, who is my fiancée's best friend, but well, he just sort of disappeared on her. So here we are!"

Cristina sips her wine slowly.

"Really, what happened with your boyfriend?" she asks.

"I don't know what to say. I came to Umbria in August and met him and kind of inadvertently fell for him. And here I am to see him, a trip we planned for four months, and he disappeared. I mean, we don't know. We think he's in Istanbul now."

Romeo smiles enigmatically and sips his Port. By the look on is face, I feel he understands very well the mercurial behavior of this Italian man.

"Why did he disappear. I can't believe this?" he asks.

"I don't know. But I can tell you this: I am done with Italian men. Done! You guys are charming and romantic... and into the opera and theater... but you are all full of bullshit. I am done with Italians!"

He laughs.

"Are you okay now? Listen, not all Italian men are bad."

"Whatever!" I put my hand up and take a drag off my cigarette. "American men aren't so great either, but at least with them, you get what you see."

"She is writing a book about it. And it's very good, so at least she got that out of I it!" Bridget blurts.

"What is the name of the book?" Romeo takes a hit off of his cigarette.

185

"*Smoke, Drink, Fuck*," I state calmly. "It's what I set out to do in August when I came to Italy, and this is exactly what I did. But alas, I don't think it has a happy ending now. In fact, I was going to write Part 2 with him during this week, but I guess that isn't happening. So I don't know if I will write the second part."

"No, you have to!" Cristina says. "Listen, it's okay if there isn't a happy ending. Women don't need the happy ending. I read that book *Eat, Pray, Love*. It was so ridiculous and unrealistic. I mean, come on, she goes to Italy, India, and Indonesia and then falls in love with some guy and brings him back to the States. Come on. Who wants to read this? It just isn't real life."

"Exactly. I hated the book too. And the movie is worse."

"So, write it. Just write it. I want to read it. Write the real story. The one all women can relate to. Here is my email address."

She scribbles it on a piece of paper.

"Your story is real. It is what women want to hear. I want to hear it."

And so there it is. These words, from a woman I barely know but will get to know later via emails and phone calls, convinces me to go forward and write when I don't even know what to write.

There is something about the power of women. They get it. They have gone through the disappointment of a loving a man who isn't what they thought he was. They support you and push you forward, even when you are in a totally different country. It seems when you think you are the only one

186

who has been through it, you encounter others who have experienced it all the same way. You are never really alone.

We go out for an after-dinner drink. Two Grappas and more intense conversation. Seven hours feel like two. Time goes by so quickly that night. Francesca insists on driving me home since she passes through Todi to Perugia. How in the hell do these people drive up and down these winding roads after all this booze? There are no cops anywhere, and it appears no DUIs are issued either.

Francesca and I talk as she barrels down winding roads in her Fiat. She tells me about her ex-boyfriends—all over the world—and how much shit they have pulled on her. She can laugh now about it. Soon she will leave Italy to return to Sweden where she will continue her research on Parkinson's Disease. She insists that I use the flight that I booked to Rome at Christmas and stay with her and her family and forget Fernando. We will have fun on our own. But right now, I really cannot bear the thought of coming back to Italy. Although I've been to this country many times before, everything about it now is associated with him. An indelible imprint lodged deep in my brain. Italy for me is now inextricably intertwined with Fernando. I can't be in Italy anymore.

And besides, I'd really be starting to look like a stalker. Perguia may not be his city, but it is located in Umbria, and these really are his friends.

"Just come back to Italy in December as you planned. You can meet my crazy
three sisters and my parents' five dogs. We'll go out every night. It will be a blast."

"I just don't think I can come back to Italy again. One day I'll come back. I'd love to meet your family and the dogs."

Anyway, I think I want to go to Argentina next. I think it's time for me to learn a language I can actually use like Spanish, and I love steak and Malbecs. It's a sexy country as well, and maybe a new adventure awaits me there. I really want to get as far away from Europe as possible. Even Spain would be too close to him.

* * *

The next day, as I board my flight in Rome to return home, I am restless and distracted at the airport, but I am not crying anymore. I am happy to go home and to have made it through this and kept my dignity. Despite my love for Italy, I do not plan on visiting it anytime again soon.

I can't sleep on the plane. My mind keeps racing. All these images of August: The waterfall and taking pictures at the bottom of the hill we hiked. Riding in the car though the countryside listening to Pink Floyd. Him in a navy blue terrycloth bathrobe sitting in his tiny kitchen under the white morning sun, a scruffy clump of black hair on his neck, handing me a white china espresso cup and kissing my hand. Rushing barefoot through open fields of sunflowers.

I have a glass of wine, and pop a sleeping pill and then another. Nothing works. I can't knock myself out. That's the thing about this trip. I drank all day every day and now my tolerance is so high, that I can't knock myself out. If I don't go on a real detox when I get home, I'm going to have to switch to heroin soon to shut this brain down.

I check my watch. Eight hours to go. Good God. I think my own mind is going to kill me. I decide to watch a movie.

I pick the wrong one. One that my mom loved and recommended—*Letters to Juliet.* It's about falling in love in Tuscany, about a love lost there and the journey much later in life to find it. I am totally captivated and stare at the beautiful landscapes I know so well. I begin to cry, and once it starts, it doesn't stop. The stoic Chinese man next to me glares at me. I spill my water everywhere. He thinks I'm a total mental patient. I *am* a mental patient. I apologize over and over, but there is no real explanation for my behavior. Ordinarily, I'd be asleep and not a nuisance to anyone but the pills haven't fucking worked.

How could I have been so strong in Italy when he was only 30 miles away from me, and now that I am on my way home to a place where I will be thousands of miles away from him, and I am falling apart? It just doesn't end.

When I finally land, there is my dad waiting for me, welcoming me home. I feel 20, not 40. The brain. The pain. It is still the same. I still need my father.

Always consistent, always reliable, he loads my luggage into the back of his SUV. We don't talk much. I welcome the silence. I don't want to talk about any of it. Not one element of this story will comport with his Midwestern sensibilities, and he was never for this whole thing to begin with. I press my forehead against the windowpane and stare again at the signs for McDonald's and Dunkin Donuts as we inch down the expressway. Eventually, I will tell him I had a good time and bought lots of cool things and brought home pesto and fresh Parma and dresses for my nieces.

"Did you see him?" he finally asks.

"No. I didn't. He wasn't even there, actually."

"Where was he?"

"I heard he went to Istanbul."

He just shakes his head. He just got on Medicare. He is old now and has been married to my mom since he was 22. He so cannot process this. And I don't want to put undue pressure on his heart. Even though I'm nuts, I realize I'm nuts and fully realize that this story is not suitable for the normals.

When I finally arrive at my apartment, I am exhausted, but I am determined to fight through the jetlag and stay awake. I unpack. I do laundry. I open stacks of mail and pay bills. I keep trying to move. I start to answer the hundreds of work emails. I am also bombarded with texts and emails from girlfriends:

"So how was Italy?"

I don't respond. They keep pouring in. It is overwhelming. And how do I explain all this?

I shut off the phone as I often do when my boss sends me his myriad mean emails, five in a row usually at two in the morning.

I go to the grocery store. I try to buy fresh lettuce and tomatoes and fish, but I can't focus. I start to throw things in the cart aimlessly. I have no appetite. Nothing looks good to me.

Then, as I am picking up a tomato, squeezing it, my iPhone buzzes. It is Antonio. "I saw Fernando today before I left for London. We had coffee, but I didn't have much time with him. I told him I was disappointed and shocked by his behavior. He told me he was overwhelmed and couldn't cope. He said it was a summer adventure, and that's all it was."

"Did you give him my letter?" I immediately write back. "How could he not be remorseful? How could he not respond to my letter?"

"I did. He got angry. He said he didn't like the part about how you said his father abandoned him and how he had done the same thing to you."

"Angry? He is now angry with me? Unbelievable!"

"I will talk to him more in December. What he did was wrong. I know what was between you. I was there. I know. It is not your fault. Please do not be upset."

I check Facebook, our only remaining connection. He has sent me a YouTube link to "Disarm," an incredibly depressing song by the Smashing Pumpkins. I click the link. I listen carefully to each depressing word.

Disarm you with a smile, And cut you like you want me to, Cut that little child, Inside of me and such a part of you, Ooh, the years burn...What's a boy supposed to do?

It is very disturbing. First of all, I hate the Smashing Pumpkins. I could smash them. They are so depressing. My sister and I once got stoned listening to them, and we both wanted to slash our wrists afterwards. And I do want to cut you. And what's a boy supposed to do? I'll tell you what a boy is to do— he is supposed to *be a man.*

And just as I am listening to this, laying on my empty grocery cart in the produce aisle, he defriends me on Facebook. The only link I have to him. Gone. (And by the way, I was planning to do this same thing as soon I got home but I only know how to do it from my laptop, so he beat me to the punch. Interestingly enough, within minutes of the defriending, he has "friended" both Daniel's sister and Francesca, who have already posted all the photos of our trip.)

I collapse on my cart right there among the lettuces. I try to stop crying, but I can't make it stop. Hunched-over octogenarians slowly pass, staring at me out of wrinkled eyes. I don't care. They can look and look and judge if they like. This guy really has cut my heart out, and he keeps slashing and slashing the remaining remains over again. I've already survived a decade and a half of breakups and bad boyfriends. I didn't even think it was possible for someone to hurt me this much—not at this age.

As I lay there on top of my cart, I do the absolute wrong thing. I call my best guy-friend Nigel. I tell him everything.

"What is wrong with me, Nigel? Truly, what is it? Why do I always pick the wrong guy? Why did he do this? Why did he just disappear?"

"There is nothing wrong with you. You are an amazing woman. Guys are just dicks. I mean, I've done this before. You know, the 'fade out' when you don't want to deal with a girl anymore."

"Are you kidding me? You've done this? What the fuck? You are 42 years old."

"Well, yeah, kind of. I mean, men are cowards. You know that. I remember this girl I dated in law school that…"

I tune out. He describes her, how hot she was, the sex, the law school classes, the dumping of her. He has said enough. He doesn't care. He then goes on to talk about his crazy wife and her spending habits and how he is really going to leave her this time. He means it this time. I've been listening to this shit for two years. Somehow it always goes back to him. Why did I call him? Why do I always go to empty wells for support?

I hang up.

I buy nothing. I abandon my full cart and leave the grocery store.

As I drive home, I pop a Xanax. I just have to stop crying and sleep, or I'm going to just die right here and now. I walk in and collapse on my bed. I cry myself to sleep and I sleep for three solid hours. I haven't eaten in 24 hours. I haven't slept properly in 48.

I am now retreating at my parents' home.

They are really busy though.

My mom is always dropping off fresh produce in the kitchen and rushing to her golf lessons. My dad is rushing to play tennis with his favorite patient, and when he comes home at night, he just watches CNN for hours. My sister is always in hurry to get to yoga and to school to pick up her kids and then hit the grocery story and the ice cream stop.

No one seems to care.

I am not the daughter they wanted or envisioned. I am not like my sister and brother, normal and settled with spouses and young children. I am a whirling dervish, full of chaos and noise and crazy boyfriends.

I open a bag of ravioli and put it in a pot. Can you believe I'm eating *more* pasta? I mean, really. But I know I have to eat something, or I'm really not going to be able to work tomorrow. And fucking meat has never produced a lick of serotonin. I need carbs.

193

As I toss them one by one into a pot of boiling water (careful not to exceed four), my father, who typically remains silent, turns to me and says, "

"You know what your problem is?"

"What, Dad?"

"Your expectations are too high. You expect too much out of men."

"Are you kidding me? Are you kidding me? I expect a guy I've been planning a trip with for *four* months to pick me up at the airport, and that is expecting too much? You are unbelievable!"

I storm out of the kitchen, leaving the pasta on the stove.

I collapse on my bed. It is late for me now. It is 1:00 in the morning in Italy. I decide I will go to bed early.

Then my phone starts to ring. I pick it up. It is Henry. He hasn't called me in a very, very long time.

I have no idea what this is about. It must be his health. He has been sick for a long time, and no one knows what is wrong with him. And as usual, I am his Florence Nightingale. Picking up the pieces. Coming to the rescue.

"Hi."

I am groggy from the Xanax and probably not going to be able to process much of what he says. I think about telling him I just popped a pill and am exhausted, but that will likely begin a litany of lectures. He does not go for pill popping. At all. He could barely tolerate my drinking.

"Hi. Are you back from Europe? I didn't know for sure when you were coming back."

"Yeah, I got back this morning."

"Oh. I see. So how was your trip?"

He knows a little about Fernando from my previous emails rubbing it in his face and my Facebook Profile picture which I immediately changed to a picture of me and Fernando in Italy. I wanted to make sure Henry saw it and duly noted Fernando's tender age. That being said, we have never really discussed the fact that I met a guy in Italy less than two weeks after he and I broke up.

In fact, I mourned the end of our relationship for all of three days and then threw myself into another one. I know this is a pattern. I do not like pain. This is why I hate exercise. I always have to pop Advil after it. I am not good at sitting with pain. I desperately want it to go away. I will do anything to numb myself from pain.

"Well, I don't know what to say about that. Things kind of got fucked up really bad with me and my Italian boyfriend. You know I met someone there. I don't really want to talk about it."

I always say that to him. I never want to talk about anything with him, and that dynamic has always worked well between us because he only wants to talk about himself anyway.

"Oh, well. I'm sorry you didn't have fun."

"I had fun. I always manage to have fun, Henry."

"Yes, you do." He laughs.

"So what is going on?" I ask.

"Well. I wanted to ask you something."

"Okay."

"My doctor in Virginia can't figure out what is wrong with me, and my blood pressure has been shooting through the roof. I have blood in my urine, and my pancreatic enzymes are high."

195

"Henry! When did this all happen?" Suddenly, I have this fear he is going to disappear too. He is going to die on me.

"Over the last two weeks, things have gotten much worse."

"You need to go to Mayo."

"I know. That's what I wanted to talk to you about. My doctor says I should have all the tests run, see all the specialists. They might be able to figure this out.

"I told you to do this last April. Yes. Go to Mayo. Just go. Do you need Jim to call someone there to get you in?"

It seems that I am always using somebody for something for someone else. I guess I am as bad as all these parasites I work with and complain about in DC. I've developed some very bad habits from that place.

"No, I think I'm okay. My friend at work knows an anesthesiologist there and can get me in soon."

"Okay. Well, let me know if you need anything."

"Thanks."

"Do you want me to go with you? Do you have anyone to go with you?"

"I think I'll be okay. But thanks. I'll let you know."

"Listen, I'm fading. I just took a Xanax right before you called."

I decide to tell him about the pill. I figure it's better to come clean because if I start slurring my words from fatigue, he's just going to think I'm drunk again and judge me even more.

And quite honestly, I don't really care what he thinks about the artifices and devices I use to ease pain. I know he is thinking bad things about me right now, but that is no longer my concern. His next girlfriend will have the pleasure of trying to be perfect and meeting his impossible standards. But I am free.

"Okay. Get some sleep. And thanks. Thanks for listening."

"No worries. Keep me posted." I hang up.

I have listened to all of his problems. I have listened carefully to every single word he has uttered about every single thing in his life. I know everything about his childhood, his family, and all his friends. I know about the ones from high school, college, medical school, and law school and today's friends too. I know about his mother and father and far too much even about his ex-wife.

I also know everything about Fernando's family. He told me all about that stuff right away. I know all his close friends in Italy—I have met them on Skype, or he has talked to me about them at length. I know about his mother and her death. I know how his father disappeared and is lost somewhere in Holland.

I once read that when J.D. Salinger wrote, he would go into a bedroom and paste pictures of the Glass family on the walls so he could imagine their lives. Every character was connected like a spoke in a wheel to someone else. I feel like I could post photos of both of their friends and family on a big blue poster board. I know *everything* about them.

They do not know my family. They know nothing about my childhood or the fact that I have often gone through long stretches of barely eating or getting out of bed. They don't really know anything about me. In fact, I have no idea why they even think they fell in love with me. But then I guess I fell in love with someone who wasn't really there.

A week later, Henry will check into the Mayo Clinic in the dead of winter right before Christmas. His ex-wife, his one person, can't go with him because she is watching the dog that they still share.

I will deal with every specialist visit. He will call me every night with a report of the day's battery of tests. I will be supportive. I will listen to him describe each and every blood test, CAT scan and MRI.

He will then say:

"And then I went to the nephrologist to have my kidneys looked at it, and the doctor was really beautiful and Brazilian and about my age, and that didn't hurt."

I want to jump through the phone and grab his throat.

I mean, he knows a little bit about Fernando, but do I ever say,

"Oh, and Fernando was only 32, and he had a big dick and could fuck like a stallion and had a full head of hair to boot."

No. I don't because that would be gratuitous and mean-spirited. And by the way, I am Midwestern, have pale blue eyes, light skin and blond hair. I do not look at all Brazilian, and he's always talking about Brazilians, including his ex-wife, who was Portuguese.

I'm so sick of this pressure to be "exotic." I mean, when did Penelope Cruz become the standard? Do you really have to be a foreigner now to be desirable? Do I have to speak Spanish or Portuguese as my first language to be cool? Please. Haven't I achieved enough by now? I don't really have the energy or interest in picking up a new language just so I can add: "Fluent in Spanish, Portuguese and French, proficient in Mandarin" to my C.V. or LinkedIn profile.

And then I think *why do I even care about the Brazilian doctor comment? Why in the hell am I even talking to him again? How did I get roped into this? What do I get out of this?*

Nothing. Nothing has changed, and he is again making me mental.

The next day, I go to work. I do what I always do. I answer the emails. I write my Department of Defense funding proposal. I interact in a positive manner with my annoying and way-too-curious colleagues. I mention nothing about the trip. I just tell everyone I had a "really good time." The older lady assistants compliment me on my new Italian clothes and tell me I look well rested. I answer every message without taking a break. I drink coffee. I skip lunch. But I'm accustomed to many drinks at lunch now. I get irritable. I go through withdrawal.

And as I manage the shakes, I get another flood of emails from my girlfriends.

"How was the trip?"

"Did you finish the book? How was Fernando?"

"Did you get engaged? I didn't see any photos on Facebook."

The messages go on and on, all day long. I throw my iPhone across the room and take a long walk in the bitter cold. It is snowing really hard and the sidewalks are icy and wet, but I just keep walking and walking. I can't deal with all this stimuli right now. And I am so incredibly tired. I just want to crawl back into my bed and sleep for two days straight. I feel the tears well up in my eyes. I can't fucking stop crying either, and I really don't want to lose it at work. That would not go over so well. My boss is a robot doctor like Henry. They don't go for emotions or drama by girls recently dumped at work.

I call Gianna, my drug rep friend, whose car trunk is loaded up like a medicine cabinet with Pfizer products. I ask her to give me a pill that will make me stop crying. I still believe that if she had just sent Pristiq for me and Geodon for Fernando last month, we'd still be together. Don't ever underestimate the power of pills. There can be much better living for humans through chemistry.

But she tells me to see a psychiatrist first before I take anything. I don't want to see a doctor. I don't want to see a therapist. I don't want to *talk*. I've done six hard-core years of therapy. I have fixed myself. He is the one who needs fucking therapy… and two or three pills a day. Not me.

When I come home from work that night, I collapse on the sofa with a big glass of red wine. I know alcohol makes depression worse, but I have to somehow numb myself and forget about this entire mess that is now my life.

And I have Christmas coming up and the third trip to live through in my head. I still have that ticket to Italy and the ones he got us for Portugal. So now I have to count down till December 23rd to not get on a plane to the country I always wanted to visit…and especially visit with him.

My girlfriends call. They text me and email me and send me notes on Facebook. They all have their opinions and two cents to offer. A shitload of unsolicited advice.

In fact, I start to think that I could write an entire piece called "I cunt deal with my cunt girlfriends." The comments that come in over these two weeks include but are not limited to the following:

- *I just don't understand this. This makes no sense. I mean, I just don't understand what happened.* (No shit. There is no explanation. Quit saying that. Why do you think I'm so f'd up from this?)

- *I don't even want to hear his name again. He is such a psycho. You are lucky it ended now rather than later.* (Okay. It's been two days and I can't even say his name again? I wish he would have punched me in the fucking face instead. At least then I'd get more sympathy and some visitors and fresh flowers in the hospital. And I'm not glad it ended sooner. I wanted to go to Portugal.)

- *He is manic depressive. He has a personality disorder. He is borderline personality disorder. He is narcissistic. He has antisocial qualities.* (By the way, when did all of you guys find time to read the DSM-IV manual and go to medical school?)

- *You didn't know him that long. Come on. You only spent a week together. How well could you have known him?* (Shut up. We Skyped. We called. We texted. We emailed. We planned three fucking overseas trips together. Yes. It was intense, but your relationship

201

moved like molasses and is totally boring. I still strongly believe in love at first sight.)

- *Do you watch Celebrity Rehab with Dr. Drew? Well, you should. They had Rachel Uchitel on there… Tiger Woods's mistress. And she's addicted to love. She is in love with love. She totally reminded me of you.* (That was from my sister. She should know I'm not like Rachel Uchitel, for Godssakes. I would not have an affair with a married man let alone a celebrity. And I would not go to rehab nor parade around in a bikini all day. And who doesn't like to be adored? To be called regularly? To have beautiful packages sent to them from Italy? If he didn't do these things, you'd say I was dating another emotionally unavailable man. She is really, really getting on my nerves.)

- *Your problem is you get caught up in these whirlwind romances and passion. That is not what it is all about. Passion fades. You just need a nice, normal stable guy.* (A guy like your husband who won't let you spend a dime and who drinks beer all weekend and watches football and tailgates on Sunday? No thanks. I want to go to violin concerts and drink champagne in Arrone.)

- *European men are different. I lived in Italy, and I always thought I wanted to marry a European, but they are different. They are romantic and charming, but really, in the end, you are just better off with an American guy.* (This from a woman who lived in Yemen for two years and schlepped a non-English speaking, uneducated carpet dealer to Massachusetts and married him—only to be divorced two years later without a prenup. Please. I do not want to hear one word from you, kettle.)

- *I can't believe you gave him all your passport information. I mean, clearly he is a sociopath. And he has all your passport information now. Does he have your social security number? Does he have your date of birth?* (Yes. He has everything. I already told you I gave him all my passport information because he had to get the tickets to Portugal! Do I really need identity theft added to my litany of worries now? Can't you see I'm already on the verge of a nervous breakdown?)

That's just a random sample. I won't even bore you with all the rest. That's the thing about your girlfriends. They are always there to pick up the pieces. In fact, they really are the only thing you can rely on in life. But they are also full of judgments and opinions and diagnoses. I don't want advice. I get it. I know how fucked up it is. I know how fucked up I am. Save your comments, please. I've heard it all before and mainly in my own head.

As the days drag by at work, things start to get more difficult. I can't stop crying when I'm driving home alone. I stop answering my phone altogether. My friend Anna texts me that she is worried about me, and begs me to please answer my phone. Well guess what? I'm worried about me too. And I really don't know what to do about that. It is like all things in life. Time just has to pass by. And then one day you forget about it. You meet someone else. It may still hurt a little when you look back on it, but it will hurt a lot less, and maybe one day not at all. There is nothing that can be done but to let the days creep by and just let time heal.

After about three days of silence, my sister calls me and asks me to come over and have a glass of wine with her. She is all about the judging and dispensing of makeshift psychiatric diagnoses. With her perfect life and adorable kids (one girl, one boy of course), she is the last person I want to see right now. But finally, I capitulate.

When I sit down and sort of begin discussing what happened, she ambushes me. Why in hell is everyone blindsiding me these days? Geez. What happened to due process? To a little notice? I do *not* like surprises. I never have.

"Listen, I don't want to upset you…"

"But you are going to, right? You are going to anyway."

"Well, I think it's kind of sweet actually. Mark my neighbor stopped by today, and I told him what happened."

"Why in the hell are you telling that weirdo what happened? Why are you telling him about my life?"

"Because! Because! He texts me all the time about you. He wants to date you, and I told him you just got back from Italy and Fernando disappeared and you were very upset and not in a good place now to date anyone."

"Oh, my God."

I bury my face in my hands. Now her crazy

neighbor knows my business. Mark, by the way, is an unemployed plumber who got dumped by his wife, has two young boys to support, and shoots animals in his backyard with bows and arrows.

"Listen, it's okay. I just wanted to be honest with him. He keeps asking me if you guys can just be friends and hang out. He wants to be friends with you on Facebook."

"He doesn't even know me." I've spoken to this guy like three times in my entire life, usually in yoga pants with my hair curly, Leif Garrett–style in a ponytail. In addition, I obviously tend to attract sociopaths.

"Well, he wrote you a card and got you these flowers." She hands me six-dozen white roses. I open the card. It's all about him—how some woman recently disappeared on him and how he, like me, is a really good person, and how devastating this is. He understands.

No, you don't. And like all men I have been with, it's all about you and your problems. I do not want to be your therapist. I do not want to talk about your Harry Houdini girlfriend. I do not want to discuss my problems with you. I do not want to be your friend on Facebook. I want to be left alone. And probably for a long time.

I don't finish the wine. I'm already sick of my sister and her crazy neighbor. I'm sure that he's going to shoot at me or tie me up.

"I'm sorry. I didn't mean to upset you. But I had to tell you. And listen," my sister whispers, "I think he's actually going to kill me with one of those arrows… not you. He keeps telling me to put in a good word for him.

I could just see him coming to my door and stabbing me with one of those arrows. Yah! Yah! Yah! I told you! I told you to put in a good word for me!"

I bolt out of there and get in my car. When my Dad later sees the roses and asks me about them, I tell him that I know he doesn't understand how I end up with these crazy men. But somehow they always find me. But, as I will later learn in therapy, penguins like penguins. We find each other.

The next day, I pick up the Pristiq again. Spinning the blue pills around and around in my hands, I decide to call the shrink. I don't want to see another psychiatrist who judges me, whips out the DSM-IV, and creates another disorder to explain my maladies. I've been in and out of them my entire life for bouts of depression. I don't want analysis or new codes on my Evaluation & Management form. I just want some fucking pills to make me stop crying. That's it.

She's late. Like all doctors are. That's why I hate them. I sit in the pristine pine green waiting room watching this makeshift Zen waterfall on a coffee table. The phones keep ringing. A teenage boy who I think may have schizophrenia sits down to me and starts rubbing his hands. This is a doctor that Gianna highly recommended, but this office is giving me the creeps. I think about slipping out and blaming it on my period or something.

Finally, her frumpy and cheerful secretary escorts me into Dr. TJ's (she goes by her initials) big office with degrees posted on the wall surrounded by orange boxy modern furniture. I feel like I'm in a gay man's apartment.

I sit down on a small white leather chair and look

over at her. She is pretty wearing sexy long black riding boots. She looks 35. At the most. When did all of a sudden "doctors" become your age, or worse yet, even younger? I feel like she and I should be friends, having coffee, shopping, chatting it up about guys and work. But here she is, my doctor. Analyzing me. Diagnosing me. Probably judging me but I don't care. I just want her to give me some pills.

I give her a glossed over version of the recent events. You know how they are—rush you in and out—30 minutes tops. She listens attentively and takes notes that I will never see unless I'm subpoenaed in some lawsuit in which case, they will all be revealed to perfect strangers.

She is Holly Hobby. Bobbed blonde hair, coiffed, polished, conservative. Talking to me slowly in a dimmed voice like I am a child with a learning disability. I hate her. She says she doesn't want me drinking. Really? Well, I don't want her quilting. "Listen, I know I have issues with depression. I know I allegedly "feel" things more strongly than other people do. I don't need you to diagnose me or analyze me. What I really need from you is a pill—something to make me stop crying, okay?"

She tells me not to drink, to take care of myself, to go to yoga, to meditate, to think positive thoughts.

Blah, blah.

Pills, *please.*

Finally! She stands up and writes a prescription for Lexapro.

"Am I going to gain weight? Just tell me. Because if that is the case, I won't take it. I'd rather suffer. I have issues with my weight. I know. You probably think that's crazy, too. I get it. Put eating disorders into your notes, but give me something that won't make me fat."

"Lexapro is weight-neutral. You should not gain weight."

She states slowly and softly.

As she writes the scrip, she tells me I should go to therapy. Ah yes, therapy. The psychiatrists answer to everything. Just talk about it all some more.

I'm not done with her yet though. She has listened to all of this shit, and she is supposed to explain to me what happened and why. I want a *real* DSM-IV diagnosis by a real doctor. I want to know what *he has.*

"The hardest thing, Dr. TJ, is that none of this makes sense to me. I'm just at a loss to explain it. I mean, I'll never ever have an explanation."

"You have your explanation. You know that, don't you?" She turns from her computer and pulls down her trendy oversized black glasses.

"No, I don't."

"Esme, he is very, very sick. From a psychiatric perspective, I can tell you he is sick. He needs help. He can't even handle his issues like an adult. And what he did to you was not only disrespectful and wrong; it was emotional abuse. You need to stay away from him. As far as possible."

And somehow, at this moment, there is a modicum of clarity and peace. All of a sudden, I feel better. It's not my friends, the makeshift psychologists, telling me this. It's a professional, an M.D. For the first time in days, I start to feel better. He *is* sick. He *is very very sick.* I like that.

Now that I realize now he is "sick" and I can't be with him no matter what, I feel great. I think of it this way—had we stayed together, we'd probably end up like F. Scott and Zelda Fitzgerald loving each other, destroying each other, writing about each other, portraying each other in the worst of lights. And just like Zelda, I'd end up in the sanitarium rocking in a wooden chair writing books that would never get published and die in a random fire.

I go back to work. I take the pills. They make me sick to my stomach. They make me tired. The crying hasn't stopped.

At night I drink red wine and eat hummus and crackers and work on my novel on my laptop. I'm barely eating. But nothing looks good anymore at the grocery store or on menus at restaurants. I have managed to shed 11 pounds... effortlessly. That is the upside to breaking up—you always lose weight and fast. I never can lose a pound when I'm happy. But despite the lack of sustenance, I have the energy to write for hours and write until two in the morning.

For weeks, the pills don't kick in. Nothing. And then... something changes. Finally. I am not crying every day anymore. I can get through the day.

* * *

Henry is at the Mayo Clinic now undergoing a battery of blood tests and EKGs and MRIs and consults. At night, he calls me and tells me again about the neurologist, the hot Brazilian nephrologist, and rheumatologist. I listen and listen. I'm starting to think he really likes all the attention he's getting there at

Mayo. I am starting to think he may have Munchausen's Disease. And because I am giving him all this attention *and* encouraging him to see additional specialists, I now may have Munchausen's by Proxy.

I say very little to Henry about my life. I don't discuss my problems. If I tell him I saw a psychiatrist and that I am exploring why I date narcissistic men, he's going to go nuclear on me and convince me that I'm irrational and making all this shit up. He knows something went down in Italy, but he certainly doesn't want to hear about the man I fell for less than ten days after we broke up. Henry is wearing me out just like he did before. He is so draining. Once again, I wonder how I got myself roped into this role. I have gone from girlfriend to mother. And I do not want to be a mother.

I go back to the shrink because she tells me I need to do so. I don't want to talk about this anymore, let alone my past relationships with men, but I'm trying to do whatever I can do to make this pain go away. I'm willing to do absolutely anything to forget him.

"You know why you met him, don't you?" The therapist asks.

"No. I mean, I thought it was sort of fate when we met, but obviously it wasn't. Obviously, it was very much not meant to be."

"Because you willed it. You said you were going to go to Italy and smoke, drink and fuck and write about it."

"I've willed a lot of things that haven't happened." I respond flatly.

"But you wanted this. You set out to do this. And he willed it too. You wonder why you two gravitated toward each other? Well. Penguins like penguins."

"What do you mean?"

"Listen, there are people out there who are wallpaper. You know who they are; I know who they are. These are people who live in the kiddie pool because that is where they are comfortable. You don't live in the kiddie pool. You never have. You live in the ocean. People like you live in the ocean because they are not afraid, and because they like it there. Fernando lives in the ocean too, and that is why you two met. He likes danger and adventure—just like you. But when you live in the ocean, you may swim over a beautiful coral reef, but you could also swim up to a great white shark that is dangerous. Fernando is the great white shark. You have to quit going for the sharks."

It makes sense, but I don't know how to process this. I don't know how to avoid the sharks.

"I didn't know he was a shark though. He was never mean to me. I told you, I thought he was the nicest man I had ever met."

"I believe you. The sharks are often very charming."

"There is something else." She continues.

"What?"

I really do want to know.

"You and Fernando were people who were both very dissatisfied with your current lives. You—with your job and your age and he with the burdens of his restaurant and loss of his business partner. You were both looking for the other person to rescue you. That never works."

"Well, he certainly didn't rescue me. He abandoned me."

"He couldn't have rescued you. Only you can save yourself."

More gobbledygook about independence and self-help.

"Do you think I can will myself a better life? To get over this, to meet the right person this time? I just don't know that I believe in that." I ask.

"I think we get what we put out there into the universe. And often you are putting things out there subconsciously."

How do I control my subconscious mind? How do I fix this and change my life and act like a fucking normal person? I hate these therapists. They tell you things that confuse the fuck out of you and make things worse.

Now all I'm going to think about is the ocean and a bunch of sea animals.

When I go to sleep at night, the scenes of him and me race through my mind over and over. Those same images etched deep into my brain. I contemplate calling a hypnotist to erase my short-term memory.

I see Fernando in the cobalt blue, untucked oxford cloth shirt the first night we met. Cutting up the pigeon on his dinner plate. Swirling the bottom of a glass of red wine. Walking naked in his bedroom and into the shower. Smoking a cigar on Daniel's balcony and kissing my cheek over and over on Daniel's front porch.

And when I fall sleep, I dream of Italy—of some amazing art collector I meet who takes me through the Uffizi museum in Florence and then shows me his private collection of art in his house. We go on long hikes, and he cooks beautiful dinners for us. I don't want to wake up. When I wake up, I run through all the elements of the dream over and over in my head.

A few days later, I will dream that I'm at dinner with Italian friends, and I go outside to make a call and am attacked by a gang of men. Suddenly, a giant man jumps out from behind a tree and kills each and every one of the gangsters. But just as he saves me from them, he cuts the scalp off the top of my head and slices out my heart. He takes my heart into his hands, then hands me back my bloody heart. I leave him calmly and go back into the restaurant, bleeding profusely and carrying my heart. I walk toward the back of the restaurant, and place it in a refrigerator. I take a seat at the dinner table, bleeding from a gaping hole in my chest, and pass the breadbasket to the guy next to me. None of my friends seem to notice my condition.

Listen, I have no idea what the hell any of this means, but I know it's weird and pretty fucking dark. I am actually starting to worry that I'm losing my mind as well as my heart. And also, there is all this fucking Italian food all over my house that he previously sent to me from Umbria. I can't bring myself to throw it away. Yet I can't bring myself to cook any of it either. I just stare at fava beans and fettuccine and Nutella. I just let it sit there.

Every day and every night, my girlfriends text or call to check in on me. And every night I sit at my small wooden kitchen table typing and then taking short walks on my deck, drinking red wine and smoking cigarettes. I gaze out onto a vast frozen lake crystallized with heaps of white snow with cylinder icicles hanging from the rooftops of docked boats. I look up at the stars and think of the summer salmon sky in Italy.

But the voices of my women friends do help at times.

It seems that many of them have been through something like this too. Men who disappear on them with little explanation. I go back to August and remember my friend Alessandra in Rome telling me that men she meets are ghosts. They just disappear. Sometimes I will talk about it with Anna or my sister, but most days I do not. But there is some peace, some real peace, in knowing other women have gone through this. Somehow, you don't feel so alone.

And this all just has to happen over Christmas.

Each day I come home from work and open a sealed white envelope with a black-and-white photo of some perfect family of some friend I haven't heard from in years—their Christmas card. They are in the Hamptons in wide brim straw hats, or Deer Valley in white ski coats and hot pink goggles. All these fucking Christmas cards. Perfect families.

Note to friends with perfect families and the Christmas cards that document the same:

Stop sending them! I don't care. I don't even know how you found my fucking address. I haven't heard from you in years. If we don't talk or see each other for years on end, we are not friends. Stop stalking me just because you procreated.

I fantasize about revenge. I was hoping next year Fernando and I would send our own holiday card, but from a safari we took in Uganda. We'd be sitting on a pristine white beach at a small table in orange-and-aqua-blue bathing suits, cradling pink champagne flutes on a small marble table, he with oversized sunglasses, me with red fingernails, leaning forward in a toast, with a tiger on my left and a camel on his right. I would blast/fax it to everyone I have known since grade school. My exotic *and* perfect life!

And also, every time I turn on the fucking news, there it is: Angelina Jolie in Lisbon.

* * *

A week later, I get a call from an ex-boyfriend's sister who used to be my boss and introduced us. This is the other anal-retentive boyfriend who I almost married a decade ago when I was turning 30. I'm still very close to his family in New York City, and she tells me that he has just died. I knew he had been sick for a long time with Leukemia, but I had no idea he was going to die, and certainly not now. I feel my heart sink. I drop my head to the kitchen table and cry uncontrollably again. I can't believe this. I can't believe he is actually gone. I think about how much I loved him and how he used to write notes in my journal and draw cartoon characters resembling us running into the woods together.

And Henry's blood pressure is going off the charts. He is back in the ER. I start to think that he too is going to die.

Then, as I turn too Facebook one day out of sheer boredom, I see that Michel, my ex-noncommittal for six on-and-off again years (during the best years of my life, by the way, which were wasted on always looking at his "potential"), has announced that he is getting married to some exotic Indian-looking woman named Preena who he has been dating for less than one year.

And my best gay guy friend George goes on

215

vacation to Hawaii with his boyfriend (posts on Facebook:

"Aloha! Just Got engaged."

I had no idea this was coming. None. And George always tells me absolutely everything. I mean they just got back together three months ago.

I want to scream out loud,

"Stop! I told you. I can't stand being blindsided. I can't be blindsided one more time. This just has to stop!"

Chapter Thirteen

It's really amazing in life how happy you can be, how incredibly and unbelievably happy you can be, and then, suddenly, in an instant, everything, absolutely everything, can change. A series of bad events, boom, boom, boom, right in a row. It can happen to anyone of us at any time. No one is immune.

You try not to be bitter. You try really hard to be grateful for your family and your friends and your job and your health, but there is a noose around your heart and a fog in your brain every day.

I start to worry that I will never, ever feel remotely normal again. I start to think that everyone is going to disappear or die on me. I feel that everything is slipping out of control.

But then one day, the fog starts to lift. Just a little bit.

Maybe it's the pills.

Or maybe it's that the statute of limitations on grief and self-pity has tolled. Maybe it's that I'm just tired of lying around watching movies on the weekend. I mean, you can only watch so much of *Welcome to the Dollhouse, Donny Darko,* and *Happiness.* You can only listen to the Smiths so many times. Eventually, depression really does get annoying even to me.

And I am starting to get fucking bedsores from lying around on the couch so much.

Somewhere and somehow, you reach for inner strength, and you find it. You pull it from places you didn't even know you had it. You are stronger than you know or could imagine.

Even though I don't know how to fix this feeling of loss or make it end for good, I know this time I'm going to lean on my pain instead of trying to run away from it. Eventually, you can only run away to so many cities and toward so many men and new jobs. Eventually, your demons catch up with you, and you just have to face them.

You can always start again. Eventually, you have to sit. And deal.

And just like that, I throw away the cigarettes, and I don't go back to them. I start running again. Two miles and my lungs are going to burst, but hey, it's a step in the right direction. I sign up for a 5K. I reroute that European ticket and plan a trip to Argentina.

I get a manicure. I buy new jeans and color my hair a shade lighter. They are little things, but they are things.

And I then I do a big thing. I quit my job.

I realize that this job—this life I'm living—isn't what I want anymore.

I know that I'm good at writing grants. I've won some big awards, and I already have one client lined up. And one client is all your really need.

So I set up an LLC. I change everything, and go forward into whole new direction.

That's the thing. When the light goes off, it really goes off. You see the bad stuff everywhere, and you realize that you just have to get rid of it. All of it.

I've always wanted my own business. I want to beat to my own rhythm. I've always been afraid to try, but suddenly, I'm not. I think this is how it's supposed to play out.

You see, when I look back on it all now, it wasn't Fernando I wanted, it was the escape from my own life. He represented the escape that I was so desperately seeking as I approached 40. And when the dream ended, it was devastating. But what Fernando turned out to be was the catalyst for major change in my life. He helped me get to where I am right now. His actions actually forced me to make a big change, and I learned to pull on the inner resources and strength I had all along. I learned to be true to myself, and I now am not trying to escape anything. It's always somewhat scary starting something brand new, but I can honestly say that on most days, I feel content. And things are going quite well, better than I ever expected.

I'm not going to tell you I started doing yoga or meditation and am really "living in the moment." Please. I'm neither that evolved nor that patient.

I'm not going to tell you that I fell madly in love and that am getting married next month. Life doesn't always end up that way. Life rarely does tie up neatly with a secure red bow over a shiny white box. It's messy and totally uncertain and precarious. Somehow though we each have to learn to live with that uncertainty and that unknown and the discomfort that it brings us each and every day. In the end, we all want to believe we can control our own destiny and have whatever we want in life. But can we?

I *can* tell you that I met a nice man who is kind

and normal and respectful. He takes care of me. He calls when he says he is going call. He isn't into text messaging, and it just feels the way it's supposed to be. He's just a smidge older than me, and he's a carpenter not a doctor or a lawyer or investment banker. He may not be what I always wanted, but I think he's exactly what I need.

And I can tell you this. As I ran in the rain and snow at seven o'clock this morning with less labored breathing, I thank God or the universe or whatever you want to call it for everything I *do* have: a warm bed, wonderful girlfriends, loving parents, a sister, a brother, two nieces, new running shoes, my health, the Postmarks blaring on my iPod, my boobs which are still relatively perky, and a business of my own that is finally starting to launch.

I mean there *always* is *something* to be grateful for, and I guess if you give thanks over and over (even when you really don't feel like it), you will start to believe, that even right now at this moment, you are a lucky person.

You probably have more than you think you do.

And now, as I look back on it, I will still say I don't regret any of it. As I said before, although I never in my wildest dreams envisioned things ending up this way, the pleasure was worth the pain. I would do it all over again because it was a wonderful experience. It was probably the best experience of my entire life.

And our experiences are God's way of teaching us something and preparing us for the next thing, right? So, let me tell you what I learned this time:

1. *Don't give up on love.*

Despite everything Fernando did, he taught me to be an optimist. I'm trying really hard to still be optimistic. I have to believe that things will, in the end, all work out as they are supposed to. And in the meantime, I'm going to keep working on me. Because I know I always have room to improve, and the more we learn about ourselves, the less likely we are to keep making the same mistakes. There is always room to learn. There is always room to improve. So I go to therapy on Wednesdays and I take ski lessons on the weekends.

2. *Give yourself some time to heal.*

It's not that easy to get over someone or something that occurs unexpectedly one random Wednesday afternoon, and it never will be. And don't let other people tell you when you "should" be over it. There is no right time. And there really is nothing anyone can say to make the pain go away. There is no way to quiet your mind. The only way over it is through it. So just sit with the pain and cry if you want to. Cry a lot. Do meth for all I care. But know that eventually, it will stop. It really will. I don't know that I could go back to Umbria now, but I know I will go again one day, and it won't hurt so much next time. And next time when I go, I'm going to buy *a lot* more sweaters.

3. *There will be no more texts.*

In my current relationship, there is only real and verbal communication. I don't want anymore "LOLs" or "TTYLs," "WTFs," "I miss U's" or whatever the next cool acronym is. Don't get me wrong. I did more than facilitate the texts—I embraced them. I too eschewed talking on the phone and embraced the convenience of text messages and emails. I too relished the barrier to intimacy that online communication provides. I get it. But I'm not doing that nor tolerating that this time.

I learned that anyone can write anything. It is a whole different thing to say it. There will be phone. And I don't care how busy you are or how expensive it is to call. There is no excuse not to call. I am going old school. Bring out the landline. Don't look at what the men write—look at what they *say and do.*

4. *Be grateful for your girlfriends.*

Today I find myself grateful for many things. But I think I'm most grateful for my girlfriends. Your girlfriends really are a gift from God. Some of them are from a past life, and some are from a new one. Recently, despite the difficulties of this trip, I connected with some old ones and met some amazingly strong Italian women who have gone through the same things as their American counterparts. I know I took them for granted. I complained about their opinions, their judgments, their constant unsolicited advice when this all went down. But deep down I know they were just trying to protect me. And in the end, it is your girlfriends who are always there by the phone, who will get you through it. We have to stick together. We women are nicer than they are. And we're all going to outlive our boyfriends and husbands anyway so we might as well start scouting for our retirement villas.

5. *Travel as often as you can.*

I will go to Argentina this year, and then I plan on going to New Mexico. And one day, I will go back to Italy. As Francesca told me many times, Fernando doesn't own the fucking country. She is right, and Italy will always have a very special place in my heart. And there are a lot of areas better than Umbria anyway. Amalfi coast, here I come.

But I'm kind of over Italy right now. As I said before, there are only so many cathedrals and chapels to see and only so many Romeos to screw. Plus, I really have got to get off of the pasta. My stomach is *still* bloated. Bring on the Malbecs and the steak.

6. *Try not to be angry.*

For many months, I have been really angry. It's good to get angry. It's part of the process. But now, I'm tired of being angry. Fernando is plagued with some real demons. He has a seed of anger in him, and if I'm not careful, it will implant itself in me and grow like a cancer. I can't let that happen. Put the anger in a container. Try to remember the good times.

I was also angry at Henry for a long time, too. But now we are (sort of) friends. We support each other. I mean, we don't talk every day, but when we are really down, we call upon each other, and we both come back to one another. We were no good at the boyfriend/girlfriend thing—we are too different and want very different things out of life. But we respect each other, and we weren't just lovers. We were also friends. There is something to being friends with your ex. I mean, just try it, if you can. (Please note, this could be bad advice as this could actually be co-dependency I am fostering. I'm still working on this one with my therapist so I'll have to get back to you.) And for the ones you can't be friends with, try to let go of the anger and be happy you found out now rather than later. I know. It's hard. I'm still working on this one.

7. *The pleasure is usually worth the pain.*

They say it is better to have loved and lost than to have never loved at all. I believe this to be true. Let's face it: Most times, it doesn't work out. It truly is so, so rare to find that one person who completes you, and to make that magic last forever. I really admire those people and hope one day I find what they have found. God. It seems impossible.

But despite all my failed relationships, I have had a ton of fun, and I'm glad I took part in each one of them. At a very bad time in my life, Fernando restored my faith in humanity... and then crushed it again. But it still was one of the best times in my life. And no one can ever take that away from me. One day, I will sit in my rocking chair showing my nieces pictures of that trip and tell them to go... to run... run to Italy. To drink wine, eat pasta, savor sunflowers and fall in love. Fall madly in love.

8. *Don't be a therapist (unless you went to school for it).*

Any guy that dumps his family issues on you on date one, two or three—RUN! It is way, way too soon for that nonsense. You will become his therapist. You will try to fix him. You won't fix him. It will drain you. You don't need to be drained. You need to be replenished. Life is draining enough.

9. *Be careful. There is nothing wrong with a little caution.*

When in a foreign country, stay in public areas. Honestly, I am actually quite lucky to be alive, if you think about it. I go hiking in the middle of fucking nowhere Italy with some random guy I met the night before while wasted in a wine bar. I mean, I easily could have been raped. (Although I doubt I could have been raped because I was so willing.) I could have been drugged and sold into some Albanian human trafficking ring, but I'm old now and I have way too much cellulite for that. If that had happened, I don't think I would have gone for more than ten dollars. My sister said Fernando could have drugged me and stolen my organs, but I suspect my liver, at this point, is the size of an Easter bonnet, so I doubt that would have fared well on the open organ market.

Anyway, the point is that I could have left Italy with a bunch of broken bones instead of a just a broken heart.

10. *Don't go Dutch.*

Just don't. Two of them have killed me now. I fell head over heels for one while skiing in Colorado on a business trip ten years ago. I never laughed in my life. He told me he loved me. He cried on the plane when we left. He then went on to marry the girl he told me he did not love. Then, this fucking debacle with Fernando—another (half) Dutchie. The Dutch are ruthless, man. During the 17th century, they killed their enemies in combat by keel hauling—basically clobbering them to death with long wooden oars stolen off shipwrecked boats. They won the World Cup. These are not people to be fucked with. The Dutch make the Enron guys look like sweethearts. And although I love Rembrandt and smoking pot in cafes, Holland, from this day forward, is off limits to me. I wouldn't recommend it to the faint of heart. Skip Amsterdam. Go to Paris or Barcelona.

11. *Love yourself.*

Cristina, the one I bummed the cigarette off of at

the restaurant in Italy, has told me this many times in emails. It didn't quite resonate, but it does now. A man is not the answer. Find your *joie de vie*. Start your own company (which is what I eventually did); write a book; take flying lessons. Do one thing that scares you. You may end up liking it. There really are a lot of things that are fun out there and will keep you happy once you get rid of the dead-end job and/or loser boyfriend.

When I look at it now, I realize that I went from Michael to Henry to Fernando all in one year, without even a month break in between. It just happened. Or I just let it happen. Maybe I was looking at them to rescue me from myself. I don't know. Believe me, I know I'm not innocent in all this. I still need to do some serious work on myself.

12. *Listen to the universe.*

Listen to the cues you are getting from the universe. They are there. You may just be choosing not to listen. I know this sounds New Age and crystals and all, but I do think there is some truth to it. When I look back on the last year, I have met a number of really impressive women who are entrepreneurs and have started their own businesses. I met a lady who quit her job as a professional fundraiser for a major corporation to raise goats and make chevre. In fact, I'm helping her now on the farm on my weekends.

Over the last year, I kept meeting these women. And now I have quit my job and started my own business. I now feel like I met these women for a reason. They helped get me here.

13. *Be true to yourself. Listen to your inner voice; it's telling you what you need to be doing.*

This one actually came from Steve Jobs, not me. But he is right.

I would be remiss if I didn't tell you what everyone is doing now. I'm happy to report, for the most part, we have all listened to our inner voices. And we are all doing knew we should be doing.

I have started my own business and have finally finished my book. Today I'm not just writing stories in my free time, I'm writing for a living. I'm finally getting paid for the one thing I love, and it seems I'm doing pretty good at it.

* * *

Ellen decided what she really wanted was that baby. She chose the girl, not the boy.

She and Daniel parted because, in the end, they just wanted different things out of life.

She adopted a beautiful girl, Emma, from Guatemala, and is loving motherhood.

Daniel, who is ready to retire and has always preferred Italy to New York, is marrying a long-term friend of his (also ready to retire) and will soon move to Todi to live a more relaxed life and eat *porchetta* at Sylvia & Pierro's.

Antonio and Bridget are happily married in London and have a little boy, Alexander, and report all good things from over the pond.

Cristina dumped that Romeo after the first date (he expected her to sleep with him that night) and met a great older man, Carlos, and started her own business—finally leaving her family's olive oil business.

Francesca returned to Sweden and made some promising inroads into Parkinson's Disease research and met an American from Texas who actually wants to stay in Sweden and not move her somewhere else.

Jackie is back home in New York and a top executive at the company (the only company) she ever wanted to work for and has a glamorous life full of perks, big bucks and international travel.

As for Fernando, he sold his restaurant in Terni, moved to London, his dream, and then decided it wasn't all that after three short months. He then moved back to Italy and was working at a small *agriturisimo* in Spoleto and living with his Cuban Communist girlfriend. Then, he moved on to another girl I think from Switzerland. Currently, I am told he is residing in India meditating. Nothing had changed. He is nomadic and not in the real world, and for sport, he chooses to wreck lives. But, I suspect he is happy now because he is not grounded in any type of reality—and this is exactly where he likes to be. I do keep wondering though when he's going to run out of money.

In the end, I think, we all ended up listening to our inner voices, and we are all in a pretty good place now.

14. *For once, don't look at the end result.*

I know this sounds cliché because I, for one, really have always been about the results. And in Italy, I learned that life is about the journey, not the destination. I know. In many ways, this is easier said than believed. But despite everything that happened and the accidental falling in love part and the desire for a happy ending part, I do believe this still. I didn't get the happy ending, but I sure had a great fucking time.

I mean how many people ever get to go to Italy, let alone have the experiences I did?

In *A Moveable Feast,* Hemingway writes about his life in Paris in the 1920s with his wife Hadley and his interesting companions, Fitzgerald, Sartre and Gertrude Stein. He refers to the city of Paris as a "moveable feast" because it is an experience, a way of life, a feast, if you will, that he can take wherever he goes.

Todi, Italy is a moveable feast, too. And I will take it with me on my next trip.

As Fernando taught me, be an optimist. There is *always* the next adventure.

And I wouldn't take anything back.

Not one moment of it.

If I could have it back, all the time that I wasted, I would waste it again.

I will do everything all over again.

About the Author

Esme Oliver has worked as an attorney, a health-care lobbyist, and a legislative director for two US Senators; work which sharpened her left brain but didn't quite fulfill her soul. Esme eventually left DC for her native Midwest, where she now writes grants (for money) and stories (for fun). She enjoys lots of travel and a long list of other activities that pair well with a nice Pinot.

Other Riverdale Avenue Books You Might Enjoy

Flashes: Adventures in Dating Through Menopause
By Michelle Churchill

Confessions of a Librarian: Memoirs of Loves
By Barbra Foster

The Secret Life of EL James: The Unauthorized Biography
By Marc Shapiro

Naked in 30 Days: A One-Month Guide to Getting Your Mind, Body and Soul
By Theresa Roemer

Shattered: The Rise & Fall & Rise of a Wrestling Diva
By Tamara "Sunny" Sytch